Merry Christmas, Miss McConnell!

Other books by
Colleen O'Shaughnessy McKenna

Too Many Murphys

Fourth Grade Is a Jinx

Fifth Grade: Here Comes Trouble

Eenie, Meanie, Murphy, No!

Merry Christmas, Miss McConnell!

Colleen
O'Shaughnessy
McKenna

**SCHOLASTIC
HARDCOVER**

Scholastic Inc.
New York

Copyright © 1990 by Colleen O'Shaughnessy McKenna.

All rights reserved. Published by Scholastic Inc.

SCHOLASTIC HARDCOVER is a registered trademark
of Scholastic Inc.

No part of this publication may be reproduced in whole or in part, or
stored in a retrieval system, or transmitted in any form or by any
means, electronic, mechanical, photocopying, recording, or otherwise,
without written permission of the publisher. For information regarding
permission, write to Scholastic Inc., 730 Broadway, New York, NY
10003.

Library of Congress Cataloging-in-Publication Data

McKenna, Colleen O'Shaughnessy.
Merry Christmas, Miss McConnell / Colleen O'Shaughnessy McKenna.
p.   cm.
Summary: A fifth-grade girl with a tough new teacher and problems
at home expects a terrible Christmas, only to have it turn out to be
one of the best.

ISBN 0-590-43554-X

[1. Christmas—Fiction.   2. Teachers—Fiction.]   I. Title.
PZ7.M478675Me   1990
[Fic]—dc   90-32176
                                                                          CIP
                                                                          AC

12 11 10 9 8 7 6 5 4 3 2 1   0 1 2 3 4 5/9

Printed in the U.S.A.   37

First Scholastic printing, October 1990

One

"I waited my whole life to get Mrs. Jackson for fifth grade and now she's leaving," cried Meg, taking a quick bite of her candy cane. "Why did she have to pick *this* year to have a baby?"

Gaelen giggled. "At least we got to have her for the first three months. That's better than never having her at all, Meg."

Meg nodded, looking up at the pink and blue balloons dangling from the overhead lights. A large cassette player next to the globe blasted out cheerful Christmas music. The whole classroom looked great! The fifth-graders had quickly decorated it while Mrs. Jackson was in the teacher's room eating lunch. When she walked through the door, the entire class had rushed forward, surprising her with cheers and baby presents.

"Did you see Mrs. Jackson's face when she

saw the room?" asked Meg. "Boy, did she look happy."

Gaelen nodded. "Wait till she sees the present we got her, Meg. It is so nice. I bet she cries."

Meg reached under her desk and lifted a large package to her lap. It looked terrific with its bright, shiny yellow paper and huge white bow. A tiny pink rattle hung from the center of the bow.

Meg ran her fingers across the rattle's smooth plastic, smiling as she remembered how nice her mom had been about buying the present last night at the mall. Even with Gaelen chipping in half for the present, Meg could tell by her mother's face that she thought the soft yellow blanket was too expensive. Mrs. Stafford had turned the price tag over and over as though she were searching for a lower price.

"Hey, no problem," Gaelen had laughed, digging into her back pocket for her mother's charge card. "I can charge it and you guys can pay me back later."

That's when Mrs. Stafford had put her arm around Meg's shoulder and given it a quick squeeze. "We'll take it," she'd announced proudly to the salesgirl. "Please gift wrap it and add this rattle."

Meg clutched the present closer and took a deep breath. Christmas was only two weeks away. So far things had been so busy at home, there had been no time for her mother and her to go to the mall together and start shopping for gifts and decorations and . . .

"Yoo-hoo, Meg Stafford, wake up!" Gaelen waved both arms in front of Meg and crossed her eyes. "Gaelen to Meg, come in, please!"

Meg blinked and then laughed.

"Wow, you were in outer space, Meg." Gaelen giggled. She tugged on Meg's dark ponytail and pulled her forward. "Come on, let's give Mrs. Jackson our present before she starts cutting the cake."

Meg and Gaelen squirmed through the crowd gathered around Mrs. Jackson in the front of the room. Even Raymond, who always tried to act like a cool kid, was elbowing kids so he could get closer.

"Out of my way, guys," he ordered, holding his present high over his head like he was wading through a swamp. "Open mine next, Mrs. J. Let the party *begin*."

Gaelen nudged Meg. "Check out Raymond's wrapping paper . . . the Sunday funnies. Don't tell me his dad was laid off again!"

Meg gasped so hard she started to choke. Gaelen turned and went red-faced as she clamped both hands over her mouth.

"Oh, Meg . . . I didn't mean *your* dad . . . I mean, I meant that Raymond's dad was always . . . but I never meant . . ." Gaelen sputtered to a miserable stop.

Meg forced a bright smile and shook her head. "I know . . . that's okay . . ." Meg narrowed her eyes and looked up at Mrs. Jackson, trying to look really, *really* interested in how the present was being unwrapped. She could feel Gaelen's eyes boring a hole right through her.

"I have the biggest, dumbest mouth," muttered Gaelen.

Meg moved up a little closer, stretching her neck to see what Raymond gave Mrs. Jackson. Raymond had been Mrs. Jackson's favorite all year so Meg knew the present was going to be really special.

Raymond was grinning and rubbing his hands together like he was about to perform a really great magic trick. "Wait till you see what *I* gave Mrs. Jackson. We are talking *great*, one-of-a-kind. . . ."

"Kind of like you, Raymond," called out Gaelen.

Meg smiled. Gaelen and Raymond always teased each other in school, but they were neighbors and really good friends most of the time.

Mrs. Jackson looked up and pushed back her short, dark hair, laughing along with the class. "I am going to miss my one-of-a-kind fifth grade, that's for sure. You guys are so wonderful to throw this great surprise party for me."

Meg stuck the present under her arm and clapped with everyone else as hard as she could. Mrs. Jackson was always telling the class how

4

nice they were, which is probably why they kept being nice.

"Look at this!" laughed Mrs. Jackson as she lifted some tissue paper and pulled out a worn green jersey from the shoe box. The name RAYMOND was printed in bright yellow letters in the center.

"Oh, Raymond, this is so nice."

"What is it?" called out somebody from the back.

Raymond stretched his neck up another inch and crossed his arms. He jutted out his chin and radiated a smug smile slowly around the room. "*That* just happens to be my good luck jersey. I hit my first home run way back in the first grade wearing that shirt." Raymond leaned closer to Mrs. Jackson and lowered his voice. "I thought your kid might like a little of the *Raymond magic* on his back one day."

Mrs. Jackson patted Raymond's curly black hair. "I'll keep this jersey with my good silver, Raymond!"

"Raymond is such a goof," Gaelen whispered. She squeezed Meg's arm. "Isn't he nutty?"

"He sure is." Meg laughed. Meg could feel Gaelen's eyes studying her to see if she was still mad about the crack about Raymond's father being out of work.

Meg smiled to let Gaelen know she wasn't mad about a thing. She wasn't. Gaelen had been her very best friend since first grade. By now Meg was used to Gaelen saying whatever popped into her head and then apologizing for the next ten minutes when it turned out to have been the wrong thing to say. And besides, Mr. Stafford hadn't quit his job or been fired. He couldn't go back to work right away because of his back injury from the accident.

Meg let a small sigh slip out. Her dad had fallen off a scaffold six months ago and his back was still not right. The doctors said he was okay, that the X rays looked fine. But things weren't fine. Nothing was really fine at the Stafford house anymore.

"Give her our present next!" insisted Gaelen, pushing Meg forward. Meg handed Mrs. Jackson the present and smiled back at her teacher.

"It's from Gaelen and me," she said proudly.

Meg and Gaelen both giggled nervously as Mrs. Jackson shook the rattle high in the air and opened the box. Right away her face softened into a huge smile.

"Oh my goodness, this is beautiful!" she cried, lifting the blanket so everyone could see it. Soon lots of kids were complimenting the blanket, saying how soft it looked and what a perfect color it was for a boy or a girl.

Meg reached over and squeezed Gaelen's hand. The blanket had been worth every penny.

"This is nice," Raymond said, rubbing his fingers against the thick satin edge. "I bet your baby will use this for his *beeba*. Man, I used to take my beeba everywhere . . . dragged it to the store, Gram's house. . . ."

"Yeah, I think I saw it hanging out of your locker this morning, Raymond," hooted Gaelen.

Mrs. Jackson slid off the desk and put her arm around Raymond who was pretending to punch Gaelen.

"Let's cut the cake before the buses are called," Mrs. Jackson suggested. "Jesse, will you help Vanessa pour the apple juice, please? Lindsay, bring the plates over, honey."

Meg's heart slipped down a notch. The last day with Mrs. Jackson was about to end. She looked over at her and almost cried. She was the nicest and prettiest teacher she had ever had.

"Time to wear your crown, Mrs. Jackson," Raymond announced. He stood on tiptoes and placed a large tinfoil crown on her head. It was decorated with green and red glitter and had five white sugar cubes that looked like jewels pasted around its center.

"Don't go," Gaelen said as she handed Mrs. Jackson a piece of cake. "You can bring the baby back here, and we can all help take care of her."

"HIM!" shouted Raymond.

Mrs. Jackson just laughed and shook her head. "I'm sure we wouldn't get too much work done with a baby crying."

"We could pass the baby around the room all day," laughed Meg.

"You can't leave now, anyway," reminded Raymond. "What about the finals for the Christmas contest at the mall next Friday? We need you to be the sponsor."

Mrs. Jackson took a small bite of cake and nodded. "I know. I just got something in the mail about that. Let me see, the finalists were Meg, Gaelen, and . . ."

Raymond made a small bow and wiggled his eyebrows. "*Moi!*"

Mrs. Jackson held up the envelope. "I have your whole skit typed, so Miss McConnell can read it. She's going to love your 'Twelve Days of Christmas.' Remind Miss McConnell to sign and return this on Monday."

A groan grew from the class. Miss McConnell was going to be their new teacher on Monday. No one had ever heard of her before.

Mrs. Jackson set her plate down and put both hands on her huge stomach, tapping her fingers. "Class . . . now you promised me you would be very nice to Miss McConnell and give her a chance."

"Why can't *she* take care of the baby and *you* come back and take care of us?" Gaelen asked.

Everyone starting clapping and whistling. Mrs. Jackson tried to look mad, but she just smiled and patted her silver crown.

Raymond hurried to the back of the room and flipped open the cassette player, putting in the Chipmunks singing "Rudolph the Red-Nosed Reindeer." Then he grabbed two pretzels and hung them on each ear as he danced around the room.

Mrs. Jackson put both hands over her ears and asked someone to please turn down the sound. She didn't look a bit mad.

Meg set down her cake and raced to the back of the room. Everyone was dancing and singing at the top of their lungs like a giant holiday had just been declared. Fifth grade was so much fun with Mrs. Jackson!

She wormed her way through the crowd and had her hand on the cassette player when a shrill whistle cut through the noise. Everyone froze in their tracks. A fire drill? *Now?* She spun around, clutching the player against her chest, the music blasting out louder than ever.

In the front of the room stood a large lady with a big silver whistle in her hand and a bigger frown on her face. It had to be Miss McConnell.

Two

"Class, I would like to introduce your new fifth-grade teacher, Miss McConnell." Mrs. Jackson was smiling and nodding her head up and down as if she were trying to be cheerful enough for everyone.

Miss McConnell stared at the silver foil crown that was sliding off Mrs. Jackson's head.

A few scattered Hello s rose from the unhappy-looking class.

"Oh, man," whispered Raymond.

From the moment Miss McConnell had blasted her whistle, the class sensed that she was in charge of the room now. Everyone took a seat, trying to swallow any last bit of cake as fast as possible. Meg practically covered the cassette player with her whole body, trying to suffocate the last lines of "Rudolph" until she could find the off button. The room was so quiet she could hear the filter bubbling in the fish tank in the back of the room.

"It was so nice of you to stop in to meet the class," said Mrs. Jackson. She looked out at the class, probably hoping to see a few nodding heads.

Meg managed a brave smile for Mrs. Jackson's sake. Actually she thought it was a little rude of Miss McConnell to just barge in unannounced and rob the last few private minutes they had with Mrs. Jackson.

Miss McConnell refused an offer of cake. She looked down her glasses at the plate as though it contained a pile of earthworms.

"I have to watch my sugar," was all she said before shoving the glasses back up to the top of her nose. She was so busy looking around the classroom, scowling at the balloons and wrappings, that she never even heard Gaelen ask her if she wanted a glass of apple juice.

Meg put her chin in her hand and leaned forward, hoping Mrs. Jackson would realize that Miss McConnell just would not work out for her special one-of-a-kind fifth grade.

Any minute she would rush forward, with her arms outstretched. "I'm sorry, Miss McConnell," Mrs. Jackson would declare loudly. "But you are not suitable for my class. I will have to stay here until I can find a better replacement."

Meg blinked as the bell rang, listening with a

sinking heart as Sister Mary Louise read the end-of-the-day announcements and sent a final fare-well to Mrs. Jackson over the P.A. system.

Meg watched as Miss McConnell stuck out her hand and shook Mrs. Jackson's. Then she turned and left with only a quick, silent nod to the fifth-graders. No, "Nice meeting you, class, I can hardly wait to get to know you." No, "I am sure that you will miss Mrs. Jackson but we will have a wonderful, wonderful year together. . . ."

Instead Meg saw Miss McConnell take out a handkerchief and wipe frosting off her fingers.

As soon as Miss McConnell left, the class rose as one and surrounded Mrs. Jackson. Everyone tried to hug her. Everyone tried not to bump her large middle. Everyone tried hard not to cry.

When the first bus was called, the children started to scatter. Mrs. Jackson followed them to the door, waving.

Gaelen stood beside Meg, tears rolling down her cheeks.

"It's never going to be the same," she announced in a shaky voice. "Monday morning is going to be the beginning of the *worst* year ever. Did you see that woman, Meg? I bet she doesn't even *like* kids."

Meg grabbed her backpack and nodded. She couldn't talk right now. If she let one word sneak out, an avalanche of mixed-up feelings would erupt.

"Good-bye, Mrs. Jackson," Raymond called

out from the door. "You're all right, you know that?"

Mrs. Jackson nodded quickly and wiped both eyes. "You, too, Raymond. Merry Christmas, children. I'll come back and visit."

Meg and Gaelen both nodded, tears welling up again.

"Merry Christmas, Mrs. Jackson," whispered Meg as she hurried out into the hall. By the time she passed the office she was almost running. Meg couldn't even imagine coming back to school on Monday and not finding Mrs. Jackson laughing and talking to a group of children gathered around her desk. She made school seem like home.

"Merry Christmas, Mrs. Jackson," Meg repeated softly.

One thing was for sure. Saying Merry Christmas to Miss McConnell was never going to feel the same way.

Three

Meg was glad to have a chance to talk things over with Gaelen on the way home.

"Miss McConnell didn't even come to meet us, not really," insisted Gaelen. "She only came for the teachers' manuals. She probably wants to give a little pop quiz on Monday morning to show us she means business."

Meg sighed. "Well, at least we have a weekend to get ready for her. Do you want to come over tomorrow so we can talk about things?"

Gaelen shook her head. "Thanks, but I can't. My mom bought these special tickets to a fancy art show, and then we are going to dinner at that new French restaurant near the museum, and . . ." Gaelen looked stricken, then slapped her hand over her mouth. "Gosh, sorry, Meg. There I go bragging again. I mean, you know I don't like going to all those expensive places, especially since your dad is . . ."

Meg bumped Gaelen with her hip and started laughing. "Gaelen, you are driving me crazy. Stop acting like you're insulting me every time you mention money. I mean, my dad is still on half-salary so it isn't like we're poor or anything."

Meg tried to keep the smile from sliding off her face. She was getting so tired of Gaelen feeling guilty every time she mentioned going out to dinner or getting tickets to the Ice Capades. Gaelen's father owned his own shoe store, two in fact, so they never had to worry about money.

"Too bad your dad had to hurt his back," Gaelen continued. "I mean, he could work in one of my dad's stores, selling shoes, except he can't bend over to look at the customers' feet. . ." Gaelen sighed. "Gosh, I wish my dad owned a hat store, or . . ."

Meg held up her hand and narrowed her eyes at Gaelen. "We are fine at our house, Gaelen. I'll see you at the corner Monday morning, okay?"

She could still hear Gaelen yelling about something as she ran down the long slope of her side yard. Little patches of snow lay on top of the frozen grass. Before she reached the front door, Buttons, her small dog, had both paws on the windowsill and was barking and wagging his whole body.

"I'm home," Meg called. She dropped her book bag and bent down to pet her dog. "Hello, you old fat dog." Meg laughed. "Gosh, we'd better ask Pop to start exercising you some more."

Buttons whined and rolled over, waving his paws in the air. Meg smiled. Buttons knew it wasn't his fault that Pop never went outside anymore. Even a dog as smart as Buttons couldn't get the leash from the hook and walk himself.

"Pop?" called Meg, She unzipped her jacket and pulled both arms out. It was last year's ski jacket and at least one size too small.

"In here," he called.

Meg followed his voice into the large dining room, and she automatically reached up and flicked on the lights. With the heavy snow clouds building outside, the room was already dark.

Mr. Stafford looked up from his seat at the dining room table and smiled. He rubbed his hand across the dark stubble on his chin and cheeks and gave a sheepish shrug.

"I didn't think it was so late. Look at me, still in my bathrobe in the middle of the afternoon."

Meg smiled, looking down at the coffee cups and plates on the table. Mr. Stafford reached out and took a bite of a cheese sandwich and then pointed to the scattered pieces of a jigsaw puzzle spread out in front of him.

"I started another jigsaw and the time got away from me, Meggie. Don't *ever* let me start another forest scene. All leaves look alike in a puzzle."

"Is Mom home?" asked Meg, as she picked up

two coffee cups and balanced an empty soda can between her wrists.

"Hey there, I can clean up, Meg," protested Mr. Stafford. But, seated in his chair, he didn't move a muscle. Instead he picked up another piece and frowned as he studied the puzzle.

Meg set the dishes in the sink and tossed the can across the kitchen to the trash basket. It missed and rattled noisily across the tile floor.

"You okay?"

"Yeah," Meg replied, suddenly feeling tired. This was the second time this week that Pop had still been in his plaid bathrobe when Meg got home from school. It made him look so old and sick to be in his pajamas like that.

She squirted liquid detergent onto the cups and sprayed water over them. Bubbles and water flew up, misting her. She stared out the window at the first flakes beginning to fall. The weather forecaster had predicted another three or four inches by tomorrow. Usually Meg would have been pleased. Mr. Stafford still had the toboggan he had had as a child, and snowy Saturdays meant forts and sledding.

"Not that we'll ever get that out of the garage again." She grabbed a sponge and scrubbed at the jelly stains by the toaster.

"I guess I'll have a boring weekend. Maybe I'll just shovel the walk tomorrow and then maybe the driveway," Meg whispered. She knew she was feeling sorry for herself, but she wanted to. It felt good, like air finally getting to a cut.

Meg moved the toaster and found another spoon, still covered with jelly from breakfast. She sailed it across the counter, glad for the rattle as it hit the coffee cups in the sink.

"Megan Stafford, what in the world are you breaking in there?" shouted Pop. His chair scraped back from the table.

"Sorry," Meg called back, running over to turn off the water. For an instant she was glad that her father's voice sounded so strong in its anger. He sounded like the old Pop. "Sorry, Pop. I guess my hands are still frozen from being outside. Did you see it's snowing again?"

The kitchen door burst open, the gusting wind blowing in flakes and Lizzie. Lizzie yanked off her hat and set a huge basket of pinecones down on the floor. "Look at all the good pinecones I found, Pop. Meg, look at this real big one. I am going to dry them off right away."

Meg kicked the scatter rug closer to Lizzie. "Lizzie, pull off your boots. Where have you been?"

Lizzie pulled off each boot and sock and then stood up and wrapped her arms around Pop. "I went to the backwoods. Pop, we can make lots and lots of wreaths, right?"

Pop hugged Lizzie back and nodded. Lizzie was only seven and always in a good mood.

"Do you have to make a wreath for school,

18

Lizzie?" asked Meg. She'd been trying to help Lizzie more with her schoolwork since their mother had started working at the insurance agency last month.

Lizzie unbuttoned her jacket and smiled even wider. "No, better than that. Pop and me are going to make real good wreaths and sell them to people for Christmas presents. We're going to make lots and lots of money, right, Pop?"

Pop took Lizzie's coat and hung it in the small mud room off the kitchen. "Right, Little Lizzie Lizard. Lots and lots."

Meg tossed the dish towel down and walked closer. Sell wreaths? Where? Surely Pop and Lizzie weren't going to walk up and down the neighborhood, knocking on people's back doors, begging them to help the Staffords out by buying a crummy little wreath!

"Go down to my workbench and bring up my hot-glue gun," Pop said. He pulled out a kitchen chair and slowly lowered himself onto it. "I'll call Mom and ask her to bring home some ribbon. Red or green?"

Lizzie clasped her hands and spun around the room. "Red — we are going to make the bestest wreaths. Meg, tell me what you want for Christmas, okay? I am going to buy Pop some new puzzles and Mommy a new shiny purse with a snap and . . ."

"Where are you going to make these wreaths?" asked Meg.

19

Lizzie grinned. "In the dining room so Pop won't have to walk up and down the stairs, and then — "

"The *dining room*?" Meg's voice swung up. How could anyone possibly put another thing in the dining room? It already looked cluttered and awful. Puzzles were flung all over the shiny dark table, and a recliner for Pop's naps, a basket filled with magazines, and a small black-and-white television had all been crowded in. It didn't look like the Staffords' dining room anymore. It looked more like a messy sick room.

"I don't think that's a real good idea," Meg began. She tried to keep her voice light so Lizzie wouldn't get upset.

Lizzie stood beside Pop and put her thin little arm around his neck. "Sure it is. Tell me what you want for Christmas, Meg. I want to buy you the first present to put under the tree."

Meg cleared her throat and tried again.

"Why don't you just forget about making wreaths and leave the pinecones in the basket, Lizzie? I think that would look great by the fireplace with a big red bow. Do you want me to tie it for you?"

Lizzie and Pop exchanged looks.

"I like Lizzie's idea about the wreaths," Pop said, reaching out and grabbing Meg's hand. "Want to sign up for the assembly line, Meg? We could always use another good worker." Lizzie and Pop laughed.

"No . . . Pop, don't you think that . . . that maybe it's not such a good idea to be . . . well, selling stuff? People might think . . ." Meg could feel the heat beginning to radiate from her cheeks. It was so hard to tell the truth when it would end up hurting someone's feelings. It was like walking across slippery stones in a creek.

Pop took his hand away from Meg's and sat up a little straighter. Meg watched as his eyebrows drew closer and closer together.

Meg knew she was about to fall into the creek.

"We don't need to sell . . ." Meg stopped. She could tell by Pop's face that he wasn't going to understand.

"So tell me what you want!" insisted Lizzie, tugging on her sleeve. "You have to want something for Christmas, Meg."

Meg looked past Pop's disappointed face and watched the white flakes blowing against the kitchen window. She knew what she wanted for Christmas, all right. And she wanted it more than any doll or toy. She wanted her mom home more often, and happy to be there. She wanted Mrs. Jackson laughing and cheerful back in the middle of the fifth-grade classroom. She wanted Pop to get out of his bathrobe and be Pop again.

More than anything, Meg wanted things to be the way they used to be. And that was something you just couldn't wrap up and put underneath a Christmas tree.

Four

"Dinner's ready!" Meg called into the dining room. When her mother still wasn't home at five-thirty, she had reheated last night's vegetable soup and sliced some cheese and salami.

"When *are* we getting a tree, anyway?" she asked. "It's almost Christmas!" She put a cup of hot soup in front of Pop. He had showered and shaved a few minutes earlier and looked much, much better.

"Yeah, can we go with the Eatons and chop down a real live tree, Pop?" asked Lizzie. "They go way out in the woods and drag it to the car and then they tie it on top and . . . ."

Pop looked interested. "Well, that does sound like fun. Of course I wouldn't be able to carry anything. . . ."

Meg slid into a kitchen chair. "Don't worry

22

about that, Pop. Lizzie and I could drag the tree, couldn't we, Liz?" Meg pushed a platter of warm rolls closer to Pop. "Do you think Mom would want to come, or should we give her a day off and surprise her?"

"Let's surprise her!" laughed Pop. "Your mother sure loves the smell of a blue spruce in the living room. She says that it smells like Christmas. She always says the tree is her present to herself."

Meg finished her soup and didn't even wait for Pop to ask before she started to make a fresh pot of coffee. Wait till she told Gaelen that they were going to go chop down their very own Christmas tree. Usually everyone went down to the Moose Club near the hospital to buy a tree.

Meg was drying the last soup bowl when she heard her mother at the front door. She ran down the hall and pulled open the oak door.

Mrs. Stafford rushed forward, both arms filled with brown grocery bags. "Hi, Meg. Grab a bag."

Meg took the largest bag and followed her mother back to the kitchen.

"Sorry I'm so late, but I thought I'd better get a few supplies in case the storm really does pass through," Mrs. Stafford said. She set the bags on the counter and smiled at the shiny kitchen.

"Thanks, Meggie. Smells good, honey. Did you remember to heat the rolls? I'm sorry I missed dinner."

Meg nodded. She could hardly wait to surprise

her mother with the tree tomorrow when she came home. Maybe Lizzie and she could crawl up in the attic and get down all the Christmas decorations.

"Did you have a nice time at Mrs. Jackson's party?"

Meg hugged her mother. "Yes. She loved the blanket, Mom. I think it was her favorite present."

Mrs. Stafford hugged Meg back and then broke away to finish unpacking. "I couldn't believe I spent so much on three bags of groceries. . . ."

"Hey, look at this, cookies are back in the house," laughed Pop. He walked over and kissed Mrs. Stafford. "Hi, honey, what goodies did you bring me today?"

Mrs. Stafford grinned and pulled out a plain-looking package of generic cookies.

Pop took the package and frowned at it. "You have got to be kidding. These taste like cardboard with plastic frosting."

Mrs. Stafford stopped smiling, took the cookies out of his hands, and tossed them into the cabinet. "They are less than half the cost of your favorites."

"That's because they don't use sugar, or flour, or . . ." Pop winked at Meg. Meg sighed, glad that the near fight never happened. Lately her parents were having a lot of *near* fights. Meg didn't like it. Even a near fight caused her stomach to clench up like a fist.

"I have some good news to share," said her mother brightly. She slid out of her coat and handed it to Pop. "I will be working at Berdine's during the Christmas rush. Plus, I will get their discount, which will help with presents."

Meg's smile faded. Berdine's? Her mother already worked at Lane's Insurance. When was she going to work at Berdine's?

"I can start tomorrow, from five till nine-thirty. Jack, make sure Lizzie remembers piano tomorrow, and Meg, can you stop on the way home from school on Monday and pick up some milk and eggs? I called the dairy and canceled the milkman, Jack. It's silly to pay extra, just to have milk delivered. . . ."

"But Gus has *always* been our milkman," Meg said. "Ever since I was a baby."

Pop pulled out the kitchen chair. "Honey, don't you think right before Christmas is kind of a bad time to cancel the milk? We always give Gus a little bonus and . . ."

Mrs. Stafford gave a short laugh. "Yes, well, *this* year I don't feel like standing on my feet at Berdine's an extra hour just so I can give the milkman a bonus, all right?"

Meg looked right at Pop, knowing how much that must have hurt him. It had. Pop's knuckles went white as he gripped the back of the chair. Then he just sort of swallowed hard like he had been chewing something tough and slowly walked back into the dining room.

Mrs. Stafford looked up from the grocery bag. Meg knew her mother felt awful about being so mean. Usually her mother never said anything like that. She was always making sure the whole family treated one another in a special way. "Treat friends like family and family like friends," was a corny saying Mrs. Stafford used to say all the time.

Meg reached into the bag and pulled out two rolls of generic paper towels and soap that didn't even have a name other than SOAP in big blue letters. She put them away without saying a thing. Meg didn't mind if they ate and used generic things, as long as her family didn't start acting . . . generic and mean.

"Mommy, did you remember the ribbon?" Lizzie slid across the kitchen floor and wrapped both arms around her mother's waist. "Just wait till tomorrow when you come home. I bet Pop and me will have a hundred wreaths all done."

Mrs. Stafford bent down and hugged Lizzie. "The red ribbon is in the backseat of the car. Put your boots on first. It's really snowing out there."

After a few long, quiet minutes, Mrs. Stafford cleared her throat and started to pour herself a cup of coffee.

"So tell me more about the party, Meg. Did you have a big cake?"

"Yes — Gaelen's mom brought in the most beautiful cake. It had a stork and pink roses with blue balloons. And Raymond gave Mrs. Jackson his old green football jersey, isn't that neat?"

Her mother blew on her coffee and smiled. "I like Raymond."

"Can Gaelen and Raymond come over next week after school to rehearse the Christmas skit? The contest is almost here and we aren't really ready. Mrs. Jackson used to help us so much."

"Sure. And I'll be glad to play the piano if you need me."

"Thanks."

Lizzie burst through the back door, her mittens and hat covered with fresh, fat snowflakes. "Boy is it neat-o out there. Meg, get your coat and come on. The snow looks like giant moths around the porch lights."

"Okay, wait till I get my boots," laughed Meg. Suddenly she was getting excited about the snow and Christmas coming. Tomorrow they would get a tree, probably decorate it as soon as Mom got home. Maybe they could even use Grandpa's old hot-dog-roasting grill and eat in front of the fire.

Meg pulled her coat from the hook and smiled. Who cared that her jacket was a little small? And even mean old Miss McConnell probably wasn't all that bad once you got to know her.

As Meg clomped down the hall to the kitchen, she could see Lizzie hopping up and down on one foot. That was Lizzie's way of showing she was really excited about something.

"Let's go, Lizzie," announced Meg. "Let's catch some snowflies!"

"Wait Meg, let me finish telling Mommy about the tree."

Before Meg could open her mouth, Lizzie rushed forward with the rest.

". . . and then we will chop it down. But Pop doesn't have to lift anything 'cause Meg and me can do that part. . . ." Lizzie paused and took a deep breath. "So by nighttime we will have a big tree in the living room . . . same as always."

Meg groaned. Lizzie had ruined the surprise. That was the second surprise that had been ruined today. First Miss McConnell coming in at the end of Mrs. Jackson's surprise party, and now Lizzie ruining the blue spruce surprise.

"Lizzie, you weren't suppose to *tell*," Meg said flatly. "I wanted to surprise Mom."

Lizzie grinned. "I couldn't keep it inside anymore. Kind of like . . . like a burp."

Meg rubbed her mittened hand on top of Lizzie's head. "I'll burp you one, kiddo."

Meg smiled up at her mother. Maybe it was good that her mom did know. She might want to tell Pop to be extra careful about driving and lifting things. Tomorrow would be his first real trip outside on his own since the accident.

Her mother set her cup down hard in its saucer, her eyes directed toward the dining room.

"I think it's a good thing that *somebody* did tell

me." She walked briskly into the dining room. "I don't *need* surprises we can't afford."

Within a few seconds Meg could hear angry voices, a fast blurred mix of shouts and whispers.

Lizzie took a step closer, and Meg wrapped both arms around her.

"It's okay," whispered Meg.

"But it isn't a *nice* surprise when it will cost me a whole day's work to pay for the tree, is it, Jack?" Mrs. Stafford demanded.

Lizzie covered her eyes, then her ears with her hands. Meg didn't bother to cover anything. She knew they wouldn't be going to get the tree tomorrow . . . or the next day or the next.

Meg pulled Lizzie toward the back door, and together they went out into the blowing snow and darkness. Meg held Lizzie's hand as they walked slowly down the driveway, both of them looking up at the snow twirling and somersaulting toward the floodlights above the garage.

"They really do look like fireflies, Lizzie. Let's call them Christmas bugs." She was glad to see a smile beginning on Lizzie's face.

"Or maybe we could call them Frosty flies," suggested Lizzie. "Or Christmas critters!"

Meg and Lizzie watched the snow fall until their feet started to get cold. And when the house seemed very, very quiet, they went back inside.

Five

Saturday and Sunday were filled with shoveling snow and helping with chores. No one mentioned the blue spruce at all.

On Monday morning, Gaelen was waiting at the corner for Meg, stamping her boots up and down. "It's about time, Meg. I was beginning to think you weren't coming to school today."

They turned and walked down Chestnut Street toward school. "I had to braid Lizzie's hair and I couldn't find any rubber bands. I finally just used old twist ties I found in the bread drawer."

Gaelen snickered. "You're really turning into a little mother at your house, aren't you?"

Meg nodded. Her mother had worked almost all of Saturday at Berdine's and spent most of Sunday up in the attic, bringing down winter clothes. Usually that would have been a fun day, listening to Christmas music, unpacking favorite decorations for the house, talking about what the family was going to be doing over Christmas break.

But this year the whole day lacked something. Meg shoved her hands deeper into her pockets and frowned. The Christmas spirit just wasn't at the Stafford house yet. Meg wondered if it would come at all this year. The only person who still sang and talked about Christmas was Lizzie, and that was probably because she was only seven and too little to realize what was happening.

"We put our tree up last night," Gaelen said. "It's huge!" She held her hand over her head. "It was so tall my dad had to chop off at least two feet."

"Save the top for us. I think that will be the closest we come to a real tree this year."

Gaelen looked shocked. "*No*, you always have a nice tree . . . that blue-looking one. I thought your mom was sort of nuts about having that same kind every year."

Meg pulled her book bag up a little higher on her shoulder and nodded. "Yeah, well, this year my mom said she isn't going to stand on her feet for five hours so we can buy a tree."

"Why can't she sit down at the insurance office?"

Meg smiled. "She works at Berdine's now, too. So whenever she talks about how expensive anything is lately, it's always, 'Finish your dinner, that ham cost me two hours of standing on my feet,' or, 'Use every bit of shampoo, I don't want to stand on my feet another hour . . .' " Meg clamped her mouth shut, hearing how awful she sounded.

Gaelen patted Meg's arm, "Gosh, Meg. Your mom was always so funny and nice. . . ."

"She still is. I mean, in between these talks about money she is the same mom. I don't know . . . I never *thought* about having or not having money before. Now it seems to be such a big deal. It's awful. Too bad I'm too young to baby-sit. I'd love to earn some money."

"Well, if we win the Christmas contest at the mall on Friday you will be rich. We all will be. First prize is over five hundred dollars worth of gift certificates. Think of all the presents you can buy with that, Meg."

"I know. I figured it out last night, and if we win, you, Raymond, and I will each get almost a hundred and seventy dollars apiece." Meg giggled. "That's a lot of 'standing on your feet'!"

Gaelen threw back her head and shot out a loud *ya-hoo!* "You can surprise your whole family on Christmas morning by having the presents all wrapped and waiting underneath the tree."

Meg covered her mouth and started to laugh. "Yeah, except we don't *have* a tree, remember?"

"Maybe Mrs. Jackson will let you take home the one in the principal's office." It wasn't until both girls ran up the large cement stairs that they remembered.

Mrs. Jackson wasn't going to be inside.

Gaelen gasped and leaned back against the red-brick building. "I almost forgot. *She's* in there . . . waiting like a mean old spider for us."

"Gaelen!" Meg laughed. "My mom told me that Miss McConnell was probably very nervous about meeting us, and she just made a bad first impression."

Galaen pulled open the door and yanked Meg inside. "I think the first impression was the *real* impression. Miss McConnell reminds me of the witch who rode her bike through the tornado in *The Wizard of Oz.* The one who hated Dorothy and Toto."

"Well, maybe we should find the Yellow Brick Road and follow it to the Emerald City and ask the Wizard to bring back Mrs. Jackson!" Meg kicked the snow from her boots and followed Gaelen up the stairs of St. James.

"Sister Mary Louise wouldn't hire a *mean* teacher," said Meg. "I think you have to be real nice and kind of holy to work in Catholic schools."

"Hah!" Gaelen snorted. "My dad said that sometimes a person is just desperate for a job, which is why they work here. Maybe Miss McConnell was thrown out of public schools for . . . for being so grumpy. And, did you see the way she ignored me when I offered her that apple juice? I looked like a real geek just standing there holding that paper cup."

As the girls neared their lockers, Raymond came rushing up. "Hey, she's here, guys. McConnell is inside the classroom, taping name tags on our desks like we were all back in first grade! And she has that forty-pound whistle hanging around her neck like she's some sort of drill sergeant."

Gaelen hurried down the hall and peeked inside the homeroom. Meg watched as Gaelen's eyes narrowed to angry slits. "She rearranged our desks without even asking. We're in *rows* now, just like the first-graders. Look at her!"

"What is she doing?" asked Meg as she caught up. Miss McConnell was taping index cards on every desk. Her name was printed in large letters on the blackboard, and both large bulletin boards on the side wall had already been changed. Instead of Mrs. Jackson's chimney scene with Santa's boot and presents peeking down the chute, there was plain white paper with black lettering reading, *What Does Christmas Really Mean to You?*

"Gosh, look. She still has one of those nerdy plastic rain hats on," whispered Gaelen. "The cheap kind they give away at bank openings. And check out those shoes! She must have been in the army before we got her!"

Raymond nudged Meg. "Why don't you go in there and ask if you can help, Meg? I bet you'd be a perfect teacher's pet!"

"No thanks," Meg answered, walking to her locker. "Besides, I don't think Miss McConnell looks like she has pets."

"Unless you count lizards and tarantulas!" giggled Gaelen. She yanked open her locker and pulled off her new green-and-pink ski jacket. Two ski tags from Seven Springs resort hung from the zipper. Underneath was a matching pink-and-green-checked wool scarf. "Like my early Christmas present? Benetton, of course, darlings."

"It's pretty," replied Meg automatically. She couldn't help but think of the early Christmas present *her* mother had given her last night after dinner. Meg sighed. The present Meg had carefully hidden in the bottom of her sock drawer this morning.

"Open them now, girls," her mother had cried excitedly, handing Lizzie and Meg each a red Christmas box from Berdine's. "More snow in the forecast so I thought you might need them now."

Meg cringed as she remembered how hot her face had become the moment she had pulled out the stiff, dark green scarf from the box. Of course, Lizzie had been thrilled with her new red scarf, wrapping it around and around her neck and spinning herself like a top in the middle of the kitchen.

"It will go nicely with your green ski jacket," her mother had insisted, staring into Meg's face. "Kind of brighten it up."

When Meg didn't say anything back, Mrs. Stafford had grabbed the box away, refolding it and frowning. "I know you wanted the one from Benetton, but I am *not* standing on my feet another two hours just so you can walk around like an advertisement. . . ."

Meg slammed her locker hard, shattering the memory. It wasn't her mother's fault. But it wasn't Meg's. . . .

"Young lady!"

Meg spun around and faced Miss McConnell. She was tapping her whistle against the palm of her hand, scowling at Meg and the locker. "Please do not slam your locker door. Try to imagine how noisy it would be if all of the students decided to do that."

"Sorry, Miss McConnell," mumbled Meg, grabbing her book bag and walking into the classroom. The classroom not only looked different, it even smelled different. It smelled like . . . like a public bathroom.

"I have sprayed the room with Lysol to help keep germs at a minimum," explained Miss McConnell. "In keeping with this policy, I expect *my* students to have a handkerchief on their persons at all times and to *use them.*" A few kids in the back snickered.

Meg slid into her seat, her eyes on Miss

McConnell. She was waiting for her to lift the whistle and scowl at the laughing children, but she let them off with a slight frown instead.

By the time the second morning bell rang, Miss McConnell already had everyone in their reading groups. Meg tapped her fingers against her workbook and tried to remember what they would have been doing right now if Mrs. Jackson were still here.

Probably having fun, talking about what everyone did over the weekend. Every morning when the second bell rang, Mrs. Jackson would always throw up her hands and make a face, telling the kids to hurry and get ready for reading before she got fired.

Meg smiled, wondering if Mrs. Jackson was having fun now. Maybe sitting on the couch reading a *How to Have a Happy Baby* book. Meg hoped she was missing her fifth-graders, too. Meg sure missed her.

"Meg!" hissed Gaelen. Meg sat up and blinked, turning to smile at Gaelen.

Gaelen wasn't smiling. Instead she pointed a low finger toward the front of the room. As soon as Meg saw Miss McConnell's face, she knew she must have already called on Meg to read.

"Sorry, Miss McConnell," stammered Meg. "I was . . . thinking."

"Whoa . . . we have a first there," teased Raymond.

"I can handle this, young man," said Miss

McConnell shortly. She tapped her long finger against her book. "Page fifty-six. . . . Could you please answer the first question for us, miss?"

Meg cleared her throat and started. It felt funny not being called by a name. Like they were all a bunch of strangers.

Miss McConnell surprised them all at the end of reading. "I think free reading is just as important as textbook reading," she began. Reaching around behind her she got a covered book.

Whenever Mrs. Jackson read to the children, she always passed out pretzel sticks and then hopped up on the side of her desk and read. Meg didn't think Miss McConnell looked like she was about to hop anywhere.

"If you have a favorite book, please feel free to bring it in and I shall consider it," offered Miss McConnell. "I am going to start with *The Great Gilly Hopkins* by Katherine Paterson."

"I love that!" blurted out Meg. She smacked her hand over her mouth and looked down at the floor. Any minute now . . .

From behind her, Meg could feel Raymond pushing his pencil into her back. "Strike two . . ." he hissed.

"Now, if you can show me you know how to maintain a quiet, orderly class, I will begin. . . ."

Meg kept her eyes on the floor until the coast was clear. Once Miss McConnell started reading, the whole class seemed to lean forward, their eyes growing larger and larger.

Miss McConnell was good. In fact, she was a terrific reader, changing her voice for every character. Meg looked sideways at Gaelen, and both girls smiled at each other. Maybe things weren't going to be so awful. Sure, Miss McConnell wasn't as young or as pretty as Mrs. Jackson, but none of the other teachers were, either. And maybe Miss McConnell had to wear those thick black shoes because . . . well, maybe she had deformed feet.

Meg leaned back in her chair and smiled. Gilly was such a great character.

When Miss McConnell finished reading, the entire class seemed much more relaxed. Meg almost clapped. Everyone was talking about Gilly and the book.

"Hey, Miss M," called out Raymond.

Miss McConnell put down the book and looked at Raymond with one eyebrow raised high above her glasses.

"I prefer 'Miss McConnell,' Raymond."

Raymond gave one of his best grins. "Yeah, well, sorry, but I was wondering if Meg, Gaelen, and me could — "

"Meg, Gaelen, and *I* . . ." corrected Miss McConnell quietly.

Raymond stopped for a second, then scratched his chin and started again. "Yeah, well, I was wondering if Meg, Gaelen, and *I* could rehearse our Christmas contest skit for the whole class after lunch. In English class, maybe."

Miss McConnell took off her glasses and pinched the top of her nose as if Raymond's question had just given her a severe headache.

Raymond grinned again. "Mrs. J — I mean, Mrs. Jackson thought we were so cool that she let us rehearse to get feedback. That means we found out if the kids thought we were . . ."

Miss McConnell pushed on her glasses and nodded. "I know the definition of feedback, Raymond. I've read your Christmas skit and the material that Mrs. Jackson left me concerning the Christmas contest, and I see nothing school-related in the entire endeavor."

"Say what?" Raymond's mouth fell open.

Gaelen and a few others laughed. Meg sucked in her breath, her eyes never leaving Miss McConnell's face.

"If you and the girls want to rehearse after lunch, I will provide a room. After reading a copy of your . . . your rap, I find it lacking in the real meaning of Christmas. However, I will sponsor you three at the contest for your skit."

"You mean you didn't like the 'Twelve Days of Christmas'?" asked Raymond. "Mrs. Jackson loved it!"

Miss McConnell just shrugged.

Galaen made a face and looked away. Meg looked down at the floor. Miss McConnell had practically spat out the word *skit.*

Meg knew the skit wasn't religious, but it was cute and it had made it to the semi-finals. Over seventy schools had auditioned, and Mrs. Jackson had been so proud of them she canceled a spelling test to celebrate.

Meg was only half listening as Miss McConnell rattled off the morning's agenda. Math, spelling, religion . . .

She looked across at the side bulletin board and its heading *What Does Christmas Really Mean to You?* and sighed, dreading that assignment. Meg would never be able to write a paper to hang on that bulletin board. This year, for the first time in her life, Christmas didn't mean a thing!

Six

During lunch Raymond wore his red Santa cap. With each chomp of his baloney-and-cheese sandwich the tiny bells on the end of the cap tinkled.

"You look adorable, Raymond," Gaelen giggled. "I'm sure the judge will give us ten points extra for you being so cute."

Raymond gave a smug smile and kept chewing. "Just so we win!"

"Did you bring the props for rehearsal, Gaelen?" asked Meg. She was getting a little nervous about the contest. It was only four days away. They just *had* to win first place and get the prize money. If they didn't, Meg didn't know where she was going to get presents to put underneath the tree. It was okay to make goofy gifts out of clay and Popsicle sticks when you were little, but once you hit fifth grade you were smart enough to know that most goofy gifts were just packed away with the Christmas decorations every year and never taken out again.

"Hurry and finish eating," ordered Raymond as he took another huge bite. "McConnell is only giving us about ten minutes to rehearse. Did you bring the cassette, Gaelen?"

Gaelen patted her shirt pocket. "Sure did. It will sound much better when your mom plays it live on the piano, Meg. Make sure she doesn't sign up to work at Berdine's Friday night, okay?"

Meg popped a grape into her mouth and nodded. She'd better make a big note and tape it to the refrigerator. Lately it seemed like her mom was trying to work as often as possible. Meg knew her mom felt better with money in the bank, but maybe it was more than that. Maybe her mom just wanted to get out of the house so she wouldn't end up fighting with Pop.

Gaelen and Raymond stood up, holding their trays. "Hurry up, Meg. I want you to hear my new rap," said Raymond. "If *this* doesn't win for us, nothing will."

Meg took a last long sip of milk and crumpled up her lunch bag. She had been in such a hurry doing Lizzie's hair this morning that she'd barely had time to pack her own lunch. Crackers, grapes, and milk. Some lunch.

"Let's get the things from our lockers, first,"

whispered Raymond as he raced up the stairs, two at a time.

Gaelen and Meg carried in the reindeer hats from their lockers while Raymond shoved both large feet into white roller skates. "Man, I hate wearing my sister's skates. Tell me if I look too weird."

He stood up, looking taller then ever in the skates and large Santa hat.

"You look great," Meg said. She bit the inside of her lip so she wouldn't smile.

Raymond skated quickly into the classroom, picking up ever more speed as he whizzed around Miss McConnell's desk.

> Merry Christmas, young and old,
> Time to see what's bought and sold
> Time to buy some Christmas cheer
> Cause Shopping Days are finally here!

Gaelen clapped. "Hey, I like that rap even better, Raymond. Let's use that instead of the old one."

Raymond skated past both girls, taking a low bow. "Yeah, I thought the owners of the stores would want to give us the prize money if we could show them how much we love to shop."

Meg sat on the edge of the desk and tried hard not to frown. Maybe Miss McConnell had been right about the skit. The rap sounded like a commercial for mall shoppers. It didn't really have too much to do with Christmas.

"Raymond, I liked the old rap where you talked about the wise men being three smart dudes who traveled far by tracking a star. . . ."

Raymond waved Meg's comment away. "Yeah, and that would really be a big hit at St. James, Meg. Sister Mary Louise would eat that stuff up. But we are trying to win at the mall so we gotta give them what *they* want to hear."

Gaelen stuck a reindeer hat on Meg's head. "Come on, his new rap is funny. We can dress up as shoppers carrying tons and tons of bags, and wear bright pink-and-green sunglasses, lots of bracelets, and look really, really rich. . . ."

Meg hopped off the desk and stuck the tape in the cassette player. "Come on, we'd better get busy. Raymond, wait over by the fish tank until your cue. Gaelen, you stand by Mrs. Jackson's — I mean, Miss McConnell's desk."

Gaelen walked over to the desk and jingled her bells. "Ready, Miss Director." Then Gaelen looked down and picked up the large silver whistle. "Hey, look. Miss Traffic Cop forgot her whistle. . . ." She put the whistle to her lips and gave a quick toot. "All right, you rude children. Get back to your seats. Make sure you don't smile in *my* class or I'll rip that smile right off your silly-looking faces. . . ."

Raymond gave the deep, low stomach laugh that he saved for really funny things. Meg smiled, shaking her head at Gaelen.

Gaelen took her sunglasses and shoved them

on her nose, sticking out her chest and crossing her arms. "Yes sir, things are going to change around here. No more of this fun-time business you had with that pregnant teacher. I mean business, and business is what I demand. Now you, Raymond, take off those skates and take off that smirk. And you, Meg. I have noticed that you haven't been paying enough attention. I want each of you to do one hundred push-ups . . . *now!*"

Meg was laughing so hard that she didn't see Gaelen's face blanch white. Or see her drop the whistle and yank the sunglasses off her face so fast they clattered across the floor.

Miss McConnell was standing, watching them. Her face was scarlet. "Rehearsal is over."

Seven

Miss McConnell stood perfectly still for a minute, then shook her head and left.

Meg looked up at Raymond and Gaelen, her face as miserable as theirs. "Wow, are we going to *get it.* I bet she's already in the office, demanding that Sister Mary Louise throw us out of here. I wonder how long Miss McConnell was standing there listening?"

Gaelen shrugged. "Long enough to hate us, I bet."

Raymond pulled off his Santa cap and shook his head. "Yeah, I don't think she's going to be asking us to water her plants or stay after school and do the boards."

Meg and Gaelen slumped into their seats. Anyway you looked at it, they were in trouble now.

Trouble big enough to last through the whole fifth-grade year.

When the other children came in from recess, laughing and out of breath, Meg tried to shrink down further in her seat. Miss McConnell marched in and put her purse in the bottom drawer, closing it with her heavy black shoe. She looked up then, giving the three a slight frown, but she didn't say a word.

Raymond looked over and raised an eyebrow at Meg. Meg raised hers back. Miss McConnell was just waiting for the right moment to strike. She probably wanted the whole class to be seated before she started to yell at them. Maybe their parents and Sister Mary Louise were marching up the hall right now to listen to how Gaelen made fun of Miss McConnell while Meg and Raymond laughed their heads off.

Meg bit into her yellow pencil, her teeth sinking into the soft wood. The silence was even worse than the yelling. What punishment was Miss McConnell planning? Maybe she would wait until dinnertime to call their parents. By bedtime none of them would be allowed out after school for the rest of their lives.

Miss McConnell stood up and walked slowly across the front of the room. She closed the door and leaned against it for a second, looking out across the class as if seeing it for the first time.

Meg took the pencil from her mouth and folded her hands, trying to look as good as possible.

Surely *laughing* at someone being rude wasn't as bad as *being* rude, was it?

Meg sighed. That kind of thinking usually didn't work at St. James. At St. James, they always made a big deal about being a leader. If one person kicks a dog and others watch and don't stop it, then all are guilty. . . .

Miss McConnell picked up her whistle and put it back on. Then she walked to the blackboard and neatly printed the assignments. Then she spent a long time dusting the chalk dust from her fingertips and finally sat down.

"When your pages are finished, please put them on my desk and start your spelling sentences from this morning," Miss McConnell announced. "When you are finished with that, you may go straight to your lockers to get ready for gym."

Meg dove into her assignments, erasing any letter that didn't look like it came off a typewriter. She would show Miss McConnell that she wasn't a bad student. She passed Gaelen as she walked up to hand in her paper. Gaelen rolled her eyes, and then walked over to the supply closet. She pulled both doors open and took out a fresh tablet, then closed the doors and started to walk back to her seat.

A shrill toot cut across the room. Gaelen yelped and the tablet flew out of her hands as though she had just been zapped with electricity.

"Young lady," Miss McConnell said in a low

voice. "What in the world do you think you're doing?"

Gaelen looked around, then pointed to herself. "Me?"

Miss McConnell walked closer, looking exactly like a cop approaching a car to give a speeding ticket. "Yes, *you.*"

Gaelen looked down at the tablet and shrugged. "I just got a new tablet. I ran out of paper."

Meg nodded her head. Mrs. Jackson always let them get new tablets when they needed one. She said they were on the honor system not to take more than they needed. Mrs. Jackson said she trusted them since the supplies belonged to the whole class and not just to her.

"If you need a new tablet, then you will come up to my desk and ask me for one," instructed Miss McConnell. "It is the procedure we will use from now on."

"Fine," said Gaelen in a tight voice. Meg had never seen Gaelen's face so red. Even the tips of her ears were turning a dull pink. She walked quickly down the aisle to her seat.

"Gaelen," Miss McConnell said softly. "If you need it, you may take the tablet."

Gaelen let out a huge sigh, almost a huff. She stood for a second with her back to Miss McConnell, then she turned around and sat down. "I don't want it anymore," Gaelen said firmly. Her eyes were almost black with anger.

The class looked from Gaelen to Miss Mc-

Connell. The whole tablet business had suddenly turned into a mean game of tennis.

"Then please return the tablet to the supply closet," Miss McConnell said just as firmly.

Meg stiffened. She wanted to rush up and pick up the tablet herself, and toss it back in the supply closet before things could get any worse. Making a big deal over a *little* thing was a sure way of getting into a fight.

Gaelen pushed back her chair with a noisy scrape and walked quickly up to the front of the room. With a wide sweep she grabbed the tablet and returned it to the supply closet.

Meg drew back in her chair, waiting for Gaelen to slam the metal doors. Gaelen's temper didn't get much use, but when she turned it on, it only had two speeds: mad and madder.

But the doors only rattled slightly. Miss McConnell was busy brushing lint from her dark wool skirt.

"Thank you, Gaelen," she said as Gaelen marched past.

Gaelen did not say, "You're welcome."

Meg opened her desk and pulled out her speller. Only a few more hours and she could go home. Usually that meant she got to relax. Now that her parents were fighting a little it wasn't quite as relaxing. But she could still go up to her room and read. Or maybe try to talk Lizzie out of selling her wreaths. The first wreath was already made and lying on the dining room table next to the puzzle. With the globs of white glue and bits of fake berries, it looked pretty bad. Meg had tied one of her best bows but it didn't help much. Lizzie and Pop were laughing and celebrating like they had just created a masterpiece for a museum. Meg shook her head. She didn't understand anybody anymore.

By the time Miss McConnell asked the class to line up for gym, Meg had finished every assignment. At least she wouldn't have any homework tonight. Gaelen was coming over to rehearse for the contest right after school.

"When you return from gym, go to the bathroom and get a drink," explained Miss McConnell. "You will find a sheet of white composition paper on your desk and a yellow sheet for a rough draft. I want you to start on the essay *What Christmas Really Means to Me* in class and have it finished by tomorrow morning. Sister Mary Louise will hang the best papers by the office."

Everyone groaned and started to complain until they saw each feature on Miss McConnell's face getting harder and harder. Soon her whole face looked like cement. She stared right back at them like she really couldn't wait until they left for gym. "Surely Christmas means something to you," she said quietly.

As the class filed out into the hall, Gaelen cut in front of two girls and stood behind Meg. She yanked gently on Meg's long dark braid. "What does *she* know about Christmas, anyway? Miss McConnell is nothing but a big old Scrooge."

Meg gave a careful nod, not quite sure if she wasn't turning into an old Scrooge herself this year.

Eight

Meg was glad Gaelen came home with her after school. On the way home they talked so much about Miss McConnell being mad at them it didn't seem as awful.

"So the worst thing she can do is call our parents or tell Sister Mary Louise, and everyone yells for a few minutes and then it's over," explained Gaelen as they walked up Meg's front steps. "I mean, we didn't tie Miss McConnell up and put her in the supply closet with her valuable tablets, did we? Besides, it's our first offense."

Meg giggled, opening the door to let Buttons run outside. The kitchen light was off and the house was quiet. In a way Meg was relieved. At least she didn't have to worry about Gaelen finding her dad in his bathrobe, all upset because he couldn't find a puzzle piece. Meg felt ashamed instantly, but shook it off. She remembered how special it used to be to bring a friend home after school. Her mother would always have an extra special snack on the table, magazines would be neatly stacked in the basket . . .

"I don't believe it!" shrieked Gaelen. She turned and covered her mouth as she started to laugh. Gaelen was standing in the middle of the living room, pointing at a small Christmas tree.

"I told you it was ugly," Meg said simply, pulling on her slippers. "I still can't believe my mother set this . . . this *thing* up in our living room."

Meg stared at the four-foot silver tree. Its outstretched tin branches looked pathetic, and even the tiny angel Lizzie had placed on top was leaning headfirst as though she wanted to jump off.

Gaelen giggled again as she tried to straighten out the angel. "Did you get this thing at a garage sale or something?"

Meg grinned. "No, it used to be my grandmother's. My mother couldn't stand it when she was little. That's probably why she loves blue spruce trees so much now. I mean, last year Lizzie found this in the attic and wanted to put it on the front porch and my mom wouldn't let her. Now the thing is in our living room."

Gaelen patted Meg's arm. "Oh, it's not that bad. Besides, it will look much better when you get a few ornaments on it."

Gaelen picked up a box from the coffee table.

"Oh, these are the felt ornaments I made you a couple of years ago. Oh, look at Mr. Snowman, and this is his wife, or girlfriend."

Meg picked up a white bird and hung it from the tree. "This bird is probably scared to be on this tree."

Gaelen hung the snowmen on another branch. "Hey, why don't we make each other some more ornaments this year, Meg?" She smiled at Meg. "I don't think we have to spend a lot of money on each other and besides, my mom always buys hundreds of craft kits when they go on sale every year."

Meg sank into the rocker and smiled up at Gaelen. Gaelen was like plastic wrap. You could see right through her.

Gaelen just didn't want Meg to worry about buying her a gift this year. Last year Meg had bought her a thin silver bracelet. And in third grade she had begged her mom until she let her buy Gaelan a red sweater to match her own.

Meg sighed and stuck out both feet, frowning at her large furry slippers. This year she didn't even dare ask her mother for ten dollars for a present for Gaelen.

"You're asking me to stand on my feet another two hours," her mother would probably say. "Just make Gaelen a card."

Gaelen sat on the floor next to Meg, pulling her feet underneath her. "I think my mom already has *tons* of craft kits, Meg. She goes nuts at the after-Christmas sales. We don't have to spend *any* money . . . what do you say?"

"I . . . I already picked something out for you," Meg started. "At Berdine's. . . ." Meg paused, checking Gaelen's face. It wasn't a lie. Meg had seen the most beautiful pearl earrings at Berdine's when she went in to wait for her mom. She didn't have any money to *pay* for them, but she did pick them out.

Gaelen shook back her thick blonde hair and let out a long sigh. "Well, I like my idea of *making* something, so why don't you see if you can return it?"

Meg lifted her huge slipper and knocked Gaelen in the shoulder. "You don't even *make your own bed*, Gaelen!"

Gaelen grabbed one of Meg's slippers and pulled it off, throwing it across the floor. Meg screamed and took off the other one, hitting Gaelen right in the face.

"Why don't we make ornaments and *sell* them?" laughed Meg. "We could travel around with Lizzie and her wreaths!"

Gaelen loved Lizzie, so she tried not to smile. "I already ordered one from Lizzie, so watch what you say, Meg. It may end up under your tree."

Both girls turned to stare at the tree, its silver sheen looking drabber by the minute. The angel's face looked stricken, as though she were stationed there against her will. "Who ever invented a tinfoil tree?" asked Gaelen.

Meg and Gaelen smiled, then snickered and finally rolled across the floor, holding their sides as they laughed.

"It's uglier than Charlie Brown's scrawny tree," gasped Meg.

"It looks like somebody made it out of leftover gum wrappers," howled Gaelen.

"Girls!" Mrs. Stafford pounded down the steps, holding her coat as she hurried into the room. "Meg, your father is asleep. Keep your voices down, please. I'm running late for Berdine's."

Mrs. Stafford glanced over at the tree, and then looked quickly away. Meg saw her mother's eyes narrow, as though the tree were an unwelcome guest overstaying a visit.

"Mom, do we *have* to have this ridiculous-looking tree in our house?"

Mrs. Stafford dug in her pockets and pulled out both gloves. "It's fine, and better yet, it didn't cost a cent." She took her car keys from the hall table and jingled them, a forced smile on her face. "Next year, a blue spruce, Meg . . . if we can . . . well, just get through *this* Christmas, we can start to look forward to next Christmas."

Meg locked eyes with her mother's, waiting for it to sink in.

Mrs. Stafford sighed. "Besides, there's more to Christmas than a tree, Meg. Surely your teachers at St. James are teaching you that. Well, I'm going to be late for Berdine's if I don't hurry. It's almost five now."

Meg nodded, getting up and giving her mother a kiss. "Sure — should I put the casserole in at five-thirty?"

Mrs. Stafford broke into a real smile and hugged Meg. "Yes, that sounds good. Three hundred and fifty degrees for thirty minutes. Make sure your father eats something. Those . . . pills are taking away his appetite."

Mrs. Stafford pulled open the door and shivered. "Lizzie should be back from selling her little wreaths any minute. Gaelen, stay for dinner if you want, sweetie. 'Bye."

After the door closed, Meg wrapped her arms around herself, shivering. Her mother was always going in or out. Always on her way to work.

Outside Meg could hear Lizzie singing. It was one of her silly make-it-up-as-you-go-along songs. Meg leaned her head against the door.

"Wreaths are good to hang on your door, and if you buy them all Pop and me can make you some mooooooooooore."

Meg closed her eyes as they started to sting. Lizzie was so good, such a sweet person. She never thought for a minute that this Christmas wasn't going to be just as special and wonderful as all the others. Lizzie was still young enough to believe that Santa would fix everything on Christmas morning, fix everything that others had left unfinished.

Meg shoved both hands in her pockets. She missed Santa a lot.

Nine

The next morning before school, Meg and Gaelen decided to wait for Raymond in the front hall. They wanted to all walk in together in case Miss McConnell was finally going to yell at them for making fun of her the other day.

Meg looked up and down the hall, watching teachers and students decorating classroom doors. Miss Duffy taught second grade and always had a picture of Snoopy on top of his doghouse with a Christmas tree perched on his stomach. Mrs. Thacker was trying to hang up drawings of candy canes colored by her kindergarteners while all the kids hopped up and down, hoping theirs would be the next one stapled to the bright red ribbon bordering the door.

"I can't believe we were *ever* that little," giggled Gaelen. "Aren't they cute?" She picked up the end of her new scarf and smelled it. "Gosh, I love the smell of things you buy at Benetton. I think they spray their perfume on it so you'll always think of their store."

Meg nodded, zipping up her own jacket so no one would notice her drab green scarf. It was soft and warm but so ugly. It was the type of scarf you gave an uncle who liked to hunt. Not a fifth-grader who already had a coat that didn't fit and . . .

Raymond came running up the stairs, his skates bouncing against his shoulders. "Well, a little welcoming committee. I like that, ladies, thank you very much. Is my coffee ready?"

Gaelen swatted Raymond with her hat. "Why did you bring your skates? You don't really think Scrooge is going to let us rehearse today, do you? Or ever again!"

Raymond looked surprised. "Yeah, well . . . she didn't yell at us or throw us out of school, Gaelen. Maybe she didn't know we were making fun of her. And besides, the contest is on Friday. If we don't get our act set, we won't stand a chance of winning."

Meg bit her lip. They had to rehearse because they had to win. Getting the prize money was Meg's only chance of being able to buy presents for her family. She had searched in every closet in the house and hadn't even found one wrapped gift so far. Maybe her mother had decided against presents this year.

Christmas without presents wouldn't be much of a Christmas at all!

"Let's all go up together and ask if we could please, please, please have rehearsal after lunch. It's not supposed to snow anymore today so we won't have indoor recess," said Gaelen. "The most Miss McConnell can do is say no and then slap us all in the face."

Meg and Raymond laughed hard as they all walked down the hall. Meg was glad to see the janitor and Sister Mary Louise lugging up the frame of the stable. They would probably finish putting up the manger scene today. Her heart brightened. Once the manger scene was set up down by the auditorium, she would start feeling that old Christmas spirit. Every year she could hardly wait for the camels, wise men, Mary, and Joseph to be in place; everyone waiting for the last day before vacation when Sister Lucille would go down to the supply room and bring up Baby Jesus.

"What are you smiling about?" asked Gaelen, nudging Meg in the side.

"Nothing," Meg said. She opened her locker and kicked off her boots, slipping her feet into her shoes. At least her mom let her get decent shoes in September and didn't force her to get a cheap pair that no one else wore.

"Oooooh, wee," sang out Raymond. He put both hands on his hips and shook his head as he stared up at their classroom door. "We have the only homeroom in the entire school that doesn't even have a measly decoration on its door. People are going to start thinking Ebenezer Scrooge lives here."

Gaelen laughed. "They'd be right. McConnell is *worse* than Scrooge. I'm not even going to give her a Christmas present. I'll mail mine to Mrs. Jackson. She's our *real* teacher."

Meg couldn't help but be a little shocked. Kids always gave their teachers *something* at Christmastime. If the teacher was boring or mean, they only got dumb stuff like cheap soap or a candle left over from last year.

"I told my mom not to even bother buying this McConnell woman a thing," added Raymond. "And I'm not wasting any of my Gram's candies on her, either."

Gaelen smiled her mean smile, the one she only used when she was plotting against her worst enemy. "Why don't we spread the word that *no one* should bring in a single present for Miss McConnell? It would be so cool. The very last day of school before vacation and not a single wrapped present on her desk. I bet she would be so embarrassed she would just quit so she wouldn't have to face us anymore. It might just work."

"Gaelen." Meg shook her head. "That's too mean."

Even Raymond looked a little nervous, like Gaelen was leading them all to the edge of the cliff with no turning back.

Gaelen rolled her eyes. "Well, come on. Don't tell me you guys like her. Miss McConnell sure doesn't like us. Did you see the way she looked at me when she caught me making fun of her?"

Raymond grunted. "Well, she wasn't supposed to compliment you on the excellent impersonation, was she?"

Gaelen closed her eyes and shook her head like she was giving up on the both of them. "Fine, go out and get her a mink coat. I don't care. At least I'm not a big, fat hypocrite. You two can do what you want, but maybe the other kids in the fifth grade will want to boycott Miss McConnell with me."

Gaelen lifted her head a notch and walked proudly into the classroom.

Raymond opened his eyes to their widest and blinked twice. "Who ever said little girls were made of sugar and spice and everything nice never met our Gaelen when she was having a bad day."

Meg grinned. She was really relieved to know that Gaelen's meanness had shocked Raymond, too. Maybe Gaelen just felt ignored by Miss McConnell. Because she was so smart and pretty, she usually ended up being the teacher's favorite. They took her stubbornness for spirit.

"Miss McConnell does seem to pick on Gaelen

more than on the rest of us," admitted Raymond. "A dangerous thing to do."

"Gaelen should just keep her mouth closed more often," laughed Meg.

Meg followed Raymond into the room. Miss McConnell was seated behind the desk, flipping pages in a book and making notations. No one was around her, talking or offering to help.

Meg felt a prickle of sadness and a thin wave of pity for Miss McConnell. Had she always seemed so gruff and mean, or did she just act that way because she wanted kids to think she didn't care if they liked her or not?

As Meg slid into her seat, she made a promise that she was going to try extra hard today to give Miss McConnell a fair chance. She didn't want to do anything drastic and try to be a teacher's pet. But the whole atmosphere in the room was getting a little tense and uncomfortable. It was getting harder and harder to get through a day without someone's name ending up on the board under REPRIMANDED.

Meg got out her reading book and sat up straight, hands folded. She practiced a smile, a nice smile that didn't look too fakey like she was trying to get away with something or being a smart aleck.

Meg looked to her left and saw Gaelen watching her. Gaelen crossed her eyes and grinned back at Meg.

It was a good sign, Meg thought. Gaelen was

out of her bad mood. Maybe she wouldn't go through with her plans to boycott Miss McConnell.

The morning bell rang and Meg was ready. Today was going to be a fresh start for the fifth grade and Miss McConnell. Meg would see to that.

Ten

Meg leaned forward in her seat during social studies, chewing on her thumbnail and nodding her head.

"The entire assassination was the result of such a sad coincidence," continued Miss McConnell in her level, low voice. "If Mr. John Wilkes Booth had not stopped at Ford's Theatre that morning to pick up his mail . . . for you see, children, Mr. Booth was a very poor actor who did not even have his own mailing address. His mail was delivered to the theater where he occasionally had a part in a play." Miss McConnell stopped for a moment. "So, Mr. Booth arrived and noticed the owner was fixing up the box seats. And what a lot of time the owner was spending. He had taken the original seats out of the box and had carried in his own settee for the

President's comfort. He was in a hurry to get everything ready for the performance."

Raymond raised his hand. "So this Booth guy didn't even know the President was coming until he just happened to walk in there that afternoon. If he didn't want his mail, he might have missed the whole thing. Mr. Lincoln would have never died that night at Ford's Theatre."

Miss McConnell nodded her head, looking very sad all over again. "Yes. It was Good Friday and the owner of Ford's Theatre knew that attendance would be down . . . with people traveling to be with relatives over the holidays. So the owner, being a smart businessman, said, 'Wait a minute. I bet if I send the President of the United States free tickets for Friday's show, then lots of people would come.' "

Miss McConnell rubbed her throat and took a small sip of water. Meg glanced around, hoping the kids wouldn't make a face the way they did sometimes. Miss McConnell never let kids go out in the hall to get drinks during class, but she was always sipping water herself.

"Can anyone tell me why people would be so very anxious to see President Lincoln? I mean, it was Good Friday and it would require most of them to change their holiday plans."

Everyone shot up their hands, waving and groaning, just like they used to with Mrs. Jackson. Meg waved hers hard, too, glad that the day was going so smoothly.

"Gaelen?"

"Because the Civil War had just ended and everyone wanted to let Mr., I mean, President Lincoln know that he had done a good job in the war."

Miss McConnell gave Gaelen a hearty clap. "Good girl. That is *exactly* the answer I was looking for."

Meg and Gaelen grinned at each other. Meg grabbed her knees and squeezed tightly. This was great. At lunch Meg would suggest that Gaelen reconsider and buy Miss McConnell a tiny gift, since she had liked Gaelen's answer so much.

"So what happened next, Mrs. Jackson — I mean Miss McConnell?" Patrick colored red and raised his eyebrows up to his forehead. He was a shy kid who barely ever asked a question.

Miss McConnell patted her stomach and laughed. "I'm big, but I'm not *that* big."

The class was church quiet for a split second before everyone started laughing. It was Miss McConnell's first joke with the fifth grade.

Miss McConnell put her hands behind her back and started walking down the aisle. "Listen to that laughter. Imagine that you are the audience at Ford's Theatre that warm spring night, listening to laughter. Remember, John Wilkes Booth had stayed at the theater all afternoon, watching two rehearsals of the play, memorizing when the loudest laugh would occur during the play." Miss McConnell stopped and looked puzzled. "Why would he waste his time doing that? We already know that Mr. Booth hated the President. He had often thought of killing him. So why would he want to hang around the theater?"

"He wanted to come and . . . and shoot him while he watched the play," Raymond answered. Raymond stopped, raised his hand, then lowered it.

The class laughed again, and Miss McConnell gave Raymond a smile.

"Sure, sure he did. Here was his chance. But why was it so important to know when the biggest laugh occurred? Was . . . was this Mr. Booth planning on writing a play or something?"

"NO," called out several students.

Miss McConnell shook her head. "Was the play *that good* that John Wilkes Booth had to watch it over and over?"

"No," the children answered again.

Now there were so many hands up, Meg didn't even have to add her own.

"Bean?"

Meg almost choked. Miss McConnell knew Maureen's nickname. When did she learn that?

"I bet John Wilkes Booth was going to, like, fire his gun while the people in the audience were, like, laughing their heads off."

"Exactly, Beanie. During the loudest laugh, Booth snuck up the stairs and opened the door to the box. He had already jammed the door earlier so it wouldn't close all the way. And . . ."

Miss McConnell held out both hands and sighed like she couldn't bear to go on. "What a pity. What a pity, indeed."

Everyone was nodding now. Meg sat back, feeling nervous and sad that the awful shooting ever had to happen.

Pretty soon everyone had a thousand questions about what happened next. Was Mrs. Lincoln shot? Did anyone from the audience try to chase after Booth?

Miss McConnell talked right through spelling class and quiz time. She didn't stop till the first lunch bell rang. She told them about the boardinghouse across the street where Lincoln was carried, and how the bed was too small for such a tall man. Miss McConnell's voice stayed low but the sadness made it even softer as she told of President Lincoln dying, lying at an angle on the small bed with his feet hanging over the edge.

When the kids finally got up for lunch, stretching and talking loudly all at once, Miss McConnell didn't even reach for her whistle.

Meg stayed in her seat for a second, waiting for the sadness to drain away before she stood up to get in line.

Meg had always known about President Lincoln being shot at Ford's Theatre. But it had never made her want to cry before.

Meg took a deep breath.

President Lincoln had never seemed so real.

It was like he had been right there in the fifth grade with Miss McConnell. She had made him real enough for Meg to really care.

Meg was the last one out. Miss McConnell flicked off the lights and nodded to Meg. She didn't say a word, but Meg knew she was feeling exactly the same way.

Eleven

It started hailing during lunch, so everyone had indoor recess after all. Rehearsal was canceled because monitors were in the room and everyone was spread out all over the place, playing board games or using the blackboard for hangman. Meg was just as glad. As much as she wanted to win the prize money by winning the Christmas contest, it was hard for her to get really interested in the raps and skits the three of them had planned. They were funny, but they all sounded like a slick commercial for some sort of fast-food Christmas. Meg tried talking to Gaelen about it.

"You're nuts, Meg," Gaelen cried. "We don't have to sing about the three wise men or dance around to 'O Little Town of Bethlehem,' do we? I mean, gosh. We want to be funny and we want to win. That's what Christmas is all about until the contest is over."

Meg slapped her hand over her mouth. *What Christmas Really Means to Me* . . . Meg had forgotten all about doing her homework the night before. Well, actually she did remember. In fact, she went up to her room to start. But then she kept getting stuck since Christmas was so "un-Christmassey" at her house this year. Meg shuddered, remembering all over again how sick she felt to hear her parents' angry voices coming up through the hot air vent. It had sounded like a swarm of angry hornets.

"Well, when *will* you be strong enough to go back to work . . . to even take a walk, Jack?" Meg's mother's voice had sounded as hard as steel. She asked the question like she really didn't expect an answer.

"As soon as I can handle the pain a little better, Jean. The doctor told me to pace myself."

Mrs. Stafford's laugh sounded like gunshot. "The doctor had no way of knowing that *pacing yourself* to you means not trying to work on a jigsaw puzzle and eat a cheese sandwich at the same time. You aren't even *trying* to get better, Jack. You are getting used to being an *invalid*. You're sleeping eighteen hours a day to hide from yourself."

Meg covered her ears all over again. She had *hated* her mother last night for saying those cruel things to Pop. But then she had covered her face when she realized that sometimes she had thought the same cruel things. Pop *wasn't* trying. He used to be so strong and sure of himself. He used to talk to Lizzie and Meg about taking life by the neck and shaking it till a person got everything she could get from it. "It's there for the asking, girls," he would declare as if he had discovered it all by himself.

"Meg, wake up!" Gaelen knocked on Meg's head and waved her other hand in front of Meg's face. "What a space cadet. You were covering up your ears, making faces . . . pretty strange, kid."

Meg stood up and hurried back to her seat. "I have to finish that dumb Christmas essay. I only have a paragraph and it's due today."

Gaelen shrugged. "I did mine in two minutes. Hey, listen to it. 'What Christmas Really Means to Me' . . . I am excited about Christmas because it means if my mother says no when I ask for lots of clothes, I can go to my dad and if my dad says no then I can ask my grandparents, and if they say no . . . I ask Santa and get it all."

Gaelen stood up and took a small bow. "Thank you, thank you. Aren't I wonderful? Thank you."

"You're wonderful all right, Gaelen. But I really have to finish this." Meg leafed through her folder and pulled out her paper. She frowned as she reread what she had written last night before she finally shoved her pillow against the vent and turned off the light and went to sleep at eight-thirty.

What Christmas Really Means to Me

By Meg Stafford

Christmas is a good holiday for families. There is nothing like a large blue spruce in the living room to remind everyone that Christmas is in the air.

Meg crumpled up the paper and pulled out a fresh sheet. She couldn't even pretend they had a blue spruce. They had a silver antenna in their living room. Meg had refused to help decorate it last night, pretending she had too much homework. She really couldn't bear to hang silver tinsel on a silver tree. The candy canes had weighed it down so much it had fallen twice. Then Pop said the tree lights were too heavy for such a tiny tree and refused to put them on because it might cause a fire. Mom said most of the good ornaments were too breakable to put on such a small tree so they were packed away. That left the felt and wooden ones. In less than twenty minutes, the only one still trying to have fun decorating had been Lizzie.

What Christmas Means to Me . . . Meg closed her eyes and tried to think. *Christmas is a time when the church is very beautiful. Sometimes grandparents come over and everyone eats a big, big dinner. . . .*

Meg stopped and chewed on her pencil. Her mother said she was waiting to see what was on sale at the grocery store before she planned the Christmas Eve meal. Usually they had shrimp and a huge turkey on Christmas Day. Meg knew the shrimp was out. And if ham was a few cents less a pound, they would have ham.

So much for tradition. She started writing.

Christmas is a great holiday. My family always has shrimp on Christmas Eve. My father insists. He says, "What good is a tradition unless you use it every year?" My mother wears a Santa apron and decorates the whole house. We even have holly on the banisters. Then we have turkey on Christmas Day, no matter what. My mother lets Lizzie and me have the drumsticks and she always takes our picture holding the drumsticks up in the air like candles. Most of all I like listening to stories about what it was like when my parents were little at Christmas. My mother and dad always kiss under the mistletoe and then laugh and pretend they didn't know we were there. Christmas is only a few days away and I can hardly wait. Christmas is worth the wait.

"Very, very nice, Meg."

Meg jumped and let out a little yelp. She twisted in her seat and looked up into the smiling face of Miss McConnell. Before Meg could hide her paper, and explain what she had written was a big fat lie, kind of a joke since the total opposite

77

would happen this year, Miss McConnell picked up the paper and held it closer, rereading it. Her smile grew larger until Meg could see every tooth in Miss McConnell's mouth.

"This is exactly what I was hoping for, Meg," she announced in a low, pleased voice. "This is what Christmas should be."

Meg watched miserably as Miss McConnell walked slowly over to the *What Does Christmas Really Mean to You?* bulletin board and hung Meg's essay in the very center.

Twelve

The hail turned to snow in the middle of science, the sky changing from white feathers to dark tar by the time the buses were called.

Meg and Gaelen laughed and clung to each other as they walked through the gusting snow on the way home. By the time they reached Meg's corner, they could barely move their frozen faces to talk. Meg had finally yanked up the green scarf from under her jacket and wrapped it around her mouth.

"Call me," shouted Gaelen from behind her pretty pink scarf.

Meg nodded, hurrying to the front door. As soon as her hand was on the doorknob, Buttons scurried out from behind the glider, his paws so clogged with ice, he limped across the porch.

"Buttons, oh, poor baby. How long have you been outside?"

Buttons let out a whimper and hung his head.

Meg frowned as she pushed the door open. She kicked off both boots and carried the snow-covered dog to the kitchen to rub him dry with a towel. Where was Pop anyway? How could he let Buttons out and then just forget about the poor dog?

Meg peered over the sink into the snowy back-yard, looking for Lizzie. Her bus was probably going to be late because of the snow. Meg frowned as she noticed Lizzie's mittens still on the counter. She had forgotten them and her fingers would be frozen by the time she got home.

Again Meg felt a flash of anger toward Pop. Hadn't he seen the mittens on the kitchen counter during his trips to the kitchen? Didn't he even *think* about getting in the car to drop them off at school?

Meg frowned, knowing that Pop didn't see what he didn't want to see. Like the piles of laundry that just seemed to grow during the day, waiting for Mom to get home.

Meg tossed a towel in the wicker basket in the mud room. There were already two baskets over-flowing. It wouldn't be long before Mom asked Meg to please start helping out with that, too. In the third grade, Meg had begged her mom to let her do the laundry. It had looked like play: adding a cup of soap, putting in the blue fabric softener, listening to the changing cycles on the machine . . .

Meg frowned at the laundry room. Sometimes *having* to do something took the fun right out of it. But someone had to do it and it might as well be Meg. She sighed and started loading the machine.

"Meg, open up!"

Meg ran to the back door to let Lizzie in. "What do you have in your hands?"

Lizzie stumbled in, dropping pinecones from her arms. Her fingers were beet-red.

"Hi, Meg, wait till you see. I found lots and lots of pinecones at lunch, and I collected them all so I could bring them home before they got all wet and gushy. Where's Pop?"

Meg pulled Lizzie in and closed the door. With one hand she pulled the tasseled cap from Lizzie's hair, letting two fat braids drop out. With the other she handed Lizzie a bowl for the pinecones.

"Lizzie, run upstairs and get into some dry jeans. Give me your wet socks and hat."

"Where's Pop?"

"Upstairs, I guess. You can wake him up and tell him about the pinecones."

Lizzie smiled wide. "Yeah, he will be so happy."

Meg got a sponge and wiped up the water, then put Lizzie's soaking socks and hat into the dryer.

In a few minutes Pop and Lizzie came downstairs, both laughing. Pop kissed Meg and started filling the kettle with water.

"So, girls, Christmas isn't that far away. Are you excited?"

Meg handed Lizzie a plate of cheese and crackers and nodded. "Yeah, I guess."

Lizzie laughed out a mouthful of crackers. "Meg, *of course* you're excited. Santa's coming. I only asked him for three things this year."

Pop laughed real hard. He carried his cup and saucer to the table and slowly lowered himself into the chair.

"Three things, Lizzie. I think that's against the law to only ask for three things."

Meg put a spoon and the sugar bowl next to Pop. When she was in the first grade, she had asked for three *pages* of things.

"Well, that's all I need, Pop," said Lizzie seriously. She took a bite of cracker and brushed the crumbs off her sweater. "I asked for a real, real easy puzzle for Pop" — Lizzie smiled across the table — "with no trees in it. And I asked for a pretty new scarf for Meg, 'cause I know she doesn't like that icky green one Mommy brought home, and . . ." Lizzie leaned forward and took a long drink of juice. "I asked Santa to see if he could bring Mommy a blue spruce 'cause I know that's her favorite, and she never even tries to smell our pretend tree even though I spray it with perfume every day."

Meg slid into the chair next to Lizzie and took a cracker. "Don't you want to ask Santa for a doll or a new bike?"

Lizzie shook her head. "No, 'cause I think I'll be big enough to ride your old bike when the snow melts. And I can work on Pop's puzzle and . . ." Lizzie laughed. "And I will take your old green scarf and put sparkles all over it and then it will be pretty."

The kettle started to whistle. Meg looked over at Pop. He seemed a million miles away, like something had pulled him right out of the kitchen so fast it left his body behind.

"Pop?"

Pop blinked, then looked at Meg and Lizzie with such a sad look you almost thought he was about to say good-bye.

Meg got up and got the kettle. Pop was beside her in a second, his cup in hand.

"Let's clear the table and play cards," he suggested. He looked over his shoulder at the snow piling up on the windowsill. "Your mom will be home soon, and we can all play cards and eat crackers till the cows come home."

Meg set the kettle down and hugged Pop tight. That sounded fine to her. That sounded just like old times.

Thirteen

School was delayed two hours the next morning, and Mrs. Stafford decided not to go to work until after the roads had been salted. For once, everyone was around the breakfast table at the same time.

Meg looked up from her plate of scrambled eggs and toast and smiled at her mother standing by the stove, spatula in hand.

"You have been smiling all morning, Meg," said her mother cheerfully. "I don't know if it's because you're missing school or if it's because my scrambled eggs are really that good."

Pop raised his coffee cup and grinned. "They're great."

Mother picked up her coffee cup and sat down next to Lizzie. She put her arm around the back of Lizzie's chair and patted her shoulder. "So, Lizzie Lizard, how many more wreaths are you going to make?"

Lizzie put down her toast, chewing and counting on her left hand. "Three, no, four, if Mrs. O'Brien is going to mail one to her daughter."

Mrs. Stafford checked her watch and then drank the last of her coffee. "Well, troops, I'll see you tonight."

Mr. Stafford got up and refilled his cup. "Don't forget to pick up the Christmas cards."

Mrs. Stafford pulled on her coat and shrugged. "Well, I don't really think missing one year is going to hurt. I can't justify spending all that money on cards and postage."

"Maybe we should send to just the out-of-towners," suggested Pop. He was leaning against the sink, already clean-shaven and dressed.

Meg watched her mother, gripping her fork and praying her mother would nod her head and say, "Good idea, Jack. I'll pick up a box and that will give you something to do during the day."

But her mother just bent down and kissed Lizzie and Meg on the tops of their heads and then grabbed her purse.

"Maybe next year," she said softly.

The car was skidding down the gravel drive when Pop opened up the cabinet and pulled out his pain pills. He pried off the cap and shook two out into his palm.

"Does your back *hurt*, Pop?" asked Meg. Usually he never started taking the pills *this* early. It wasn't even ten o'clock yet.

Lizzie hopped off her chair and poured the milk from her cereal into the sink. "I think Santa should bring you a new back, Pop. A strong kind, like you used to have."

Pop gave a half laugh, half grunt from behind his glass of water.

"Come on, Lizzie. I'll walk you to your bus stop," offered Meg.

"How come *I* can't walk to school like you and Gaelen?" asked Lizzie, dragging both boots out from the mud room.

"It's too far for you," answered Meg. She dropped Lizzie's red jacket and matching mittens on the floor next to her. "And don't forget your mittens today."

Lizzie kissed Pop and grabbed her lunch from the counter. "Pop, can we build a snow fort with all this good snow when I get home from school? Vanessa's dad built her one with a window and a little seat."

Pop crossed his arms and nodded. "Sure. Maybe your fort can even have an outdoor swimming pool."

Meg laughed. "Are you really going to go outside, Pop?"

"Sure," Pop reached up and rubbed his back. "I think I'd better start trying to tackle a few more things. I'm getting a little bored with puzzles. I guess I'm getting cabin fever. Maybe I'll give Mr. Edwards a call and see what's going on at work."

Meg kept grinning at her dad until she walked out the front door. Maybe the fight the other night had helped a little bit. Maybe it woke Pop up and hurt his feelings enough to realize that other people's feelings were getting pretty stepped on, too.

Suddenly Meg felt a burst of energy inside. Maybe it was her own Christmas spirit waking up. "Pop, the Christmas contest is this Friday at the mall. Are you going to come? Then we can pick Mom up at Berdine's and all four of us can walk around the mall and see the Christmas decorations."

"Sounds good," Pop agreed. He handed Meg her green scarf and gloves. "Stay warm, girls. I'll be waiting with the shovels when you get home from school. I thought you could shovel the walk and driveway for me and then maybe we'll all go get Mom that blue spruce she's been wanting."

"What?" Lizzie and Meg started laughing and hopping up and down around Pop.

"Hey, I'm surrounded," shouted Pop. He held up a dish towel and swatted at them both.

"But . . . but Mom said they were . . ." Meg stopped. Was Pop forgetting that the blue spruce trees were so expensive?

Pop shook his head and opened the door. "Out, out. You let your old man worry about the price tag for a change. The Staffords have always had a blue spruce in their front room. What good is a tradition unless you use it every year?"

Meg grabbed her book bag and then Lizzie's hand. As a special treat she let Lizzie walk all the way to school with her and Gaelen.

Meg was talking so fast about the blue spruce and getting the good decorations back down from the attic, she didn't even realize her green scarf was outside her jacket, flapping in the wind.

Fourteen

When Gaelen and Meg walked into the classroom, there were three or four kids around Miss
McConnell's desk. Patrick Frank was showing a
model of a plane he had just finished.

"Hi, Miss McConnell," Meg said cheerfully.
She slid into her seat and got out a sheet of paper.
Lizzie would really be happy if Meg came home
with a Christmas list. Meg took out a green
marker and made a small number 1. *new colored
pencils and pad.* Meg erased "pad" and made that
number 2. It would be better if the list looked
longer. Meg chewed the end of her eraser and
thought. What did she want that didn't cost too
much?

Number 3: cherry-flavored Chap Stick
Number 4: new white knee socks
Meg sighed and erased number 4. It would only

remind her mother how Meg ruined the laundry yesterday by washing the red sweatshirt with the underwear. She stuck out her leg and shook her head at the pink sock.

"Excuse me, Miss . . ." Meg looked up and saw Gaelen in front of her, smiling and holding her hair away from each ear. "Notice anything different about *moi*?"

Gaelen shook back her hair and twirled around, each arm extended in a graceful arc.

"Something wrong with your arms?" asked Meg. "Your elbows are locked in that position?"

Gaelen dropped her arms and leaned closer. "My ears, dummy. Look . . . my mother let me get one ear double-pierced last night. Can you believe it?"

Meg couldn't. Gaelen had been begging her mom for three months to let her get at least *one* ear double-pierced. But the answer had always been, "No, that looks too cheap."

Gaelen perched on the end of Meg's desk. "Mom and I went shopping last night . . . by the way, we stopped in to see your mom at Berdine's, and she was really good at helping people, so anyway, this lady in a Santa suit was double-piercing and all the money was going to go to the hospital so my mom said, 'Why not?' We had so much fun!"

Gaelen reached up and touched the tiny gold ball. "I think I look at least fourteen now."

Meg glanced back down at her list. Maybe she should add "double-piercing."

The morning bell rang just as Raymond was slipping in through the door. He was panting and his tie was crooked. He held up one hand as a salute to Miss McConnell and slipped into his seat behind Meg.

"You were almost tardy," Meg laughed, twisting around in her seat. "Did you miss the bus?"

Raymond didn't smile back. He just shook his head and tried to catch his breath. "I . . . my mom said I should bring in some of Gram's homemade candy for Miss McConnell, since she's my teacher. I had to stop by Gram's on the way and pick it up before Gram left for vacation."

"Raymond, that's so nice." Meg could see that Raymond was a little embarrassed. But he must have wanted to give Miss McConnell the present or he would have just let his older sister, Shemmie, bring it in.

"Where is it?"

Raymond jerked his thumb toward the door. "In my locker. I'll give it to her at lunch, I guess. I guess Gaelen has called off her boycott, anyway."

Meg twisted back around feeling better than ever. There really must be something magical about Christmas. Good things seemed to multiply. And maybe since things were starting to go so well, they might just win first prize at the mall Christmas contest on Friday night, too.

In the middle of math, a second-grader came in with a message for Miss McConnell. Miss McConnell read it and announced that since Friday would be the last day of school before Christmas vacation, there would be a Mass at nine-thirty. All parents were welcome to attend and there would be a reception following, with the sixth-graders presenting a program.

Meg nodded, sure that Pop would want to come. Her mother had to work, but maybe she could ask if she could come in late. Mrs. Stafford had never missed the Christmas Mass before. She usually cried when the little first-graders carried up their offerings for Baby Jesus. They were just cans of beans and soup for the poor people in the parish, but by the time the kindergarteners read their prayers for peace, Mrs. Stafford was usually on her second tissue.

Miss McConnell snapped shut the math book and checked her watch. "Class, I have to run down to the office for a minute. Please finish correcting your math, and for those of you who have already finished, you may free read."

Meg picked up her pencil and looked at the last problem. If she hurried, she would have time to finish her Christmas list and give it to Lizzie during school. Meg giggled, thinking how much fun it would be to surprise Lizzie and leave the list in her locker.

"Gaelen — would you be in charge for the next five minutes, please?" asked Miss McConnell. Gaelen walked to the front of the room and sat behind Miss McConnell's desk. Meg looked up, waiting for Gaelen to put on Miss McConnell's glasses, or make a funny face.

But Gaelen just sat there, doing her math and looking up from time to time to make sure everyone was being good.

"Hey, Meg . . ." Raymond tugged on Meg's ponytail.

"What?" hissed Meg.

"Look what I found in my locker." Raymond knocked on her shoulder and tossed a folded sheet of paper on top of Meg's desk. "Man, I can't believe I wrote this. I guess it was when Miss McConnell was being such a Scrooge. Read it and then rip it up."

Meg lowered the white square to her lap and carefully unfolded it, grimacing with each crinkling sound. Passing notes was really frowned on at St. James. "Always be proud enough of your thoughts to say them aloud!"

There were two poems printed neatly. The first one was the rap Raymond had written for the Christmas contest. It was pretty funny.

On the first day of Christmas, my true
love gave to me . . .
A Swatch watch and a Sony.

On the second day of Christmas, my
true love gave to me . . .
Two racing cars, and a Swatch watch
and a Sony . . .

Meg put her hand over her mouth and giggled,
remembering how many props they were going
to have to bring to the mall to do this song. By
the end of the song all three of them would have
their arms filled with presents and then Raymond
would pretend to collapse when Meg handed him
a tiny candy cane. Maybe they had a chance of
winning after all.

Down at the bottom of the page, Raymond had
added something else in black Magic Marker. The
whole poem was surrounded by frowning faces.

Fee, fie, fiddle dee-ooh
This McConnell chick has got to go!!
She's news too bad to print or say,
She's the witch of the east and she's
in my way. . . .

Meg lowered the page, her face getting warm.
She felt guilty all over again for the rude com-
ments they had all made about Miss McConnell
earlier. Of course, she was a little grumpy then.
But now she was so nice to everyone. The kids
really seemed to like her a lot better.

"Get rid of it, man," Raymond ordered
hoarsely.

Meg didn't even finish reading it. The rap went on and on for another four verses. Meg caught the phrase "whistle stuck in her fat face," and knew she didn't really want to read any more.

She slid out of her seat, folding the note in half. She didn't want to keep it in her desk. The sooner she could rip it into a thousand pieces, the better.

Meg walked up to the trash can.

Gaelen looked up and Meg could tell by her grin that she was going to do something dumb.

"Excuse me, Miss Stafford, but I don't believe you asked *permission* to *leave* your seat. Please return to it and raise your hand."

A few kids giggled.

Meg lowered her voice, keeping one eye on the closed door. Now was *not* the time for jokes.

"I have to get rid of this," she said between clenched teeth.

"Your teeth are locked together?" asked Gaelen cheerfully. "Is that what you're trying to say?"

Meg sighed and held up the note. "I've got to get *rid of this*!" she snapped.

Gaelen leaned back in her chair. and raised both eyebrows. "Well, EXCUSE ME!"

Meg grinned. Gosh, you practically had to hit Gaelen over the head to . . .

"Let me see that first," snapped Gaelen, reaching over and taking it. "I am in charge, Miss Stafford." Gaelen skimmed the note laughing, and then growing serious. Her face grew pink.

"Don't . . ." Meg stretched out across the desk,

grabbing again for the note. Her elbow hit the glass of water by Miss McConnell's pencil can and knocked it right down.

"Meg!" cried Gaelen, jumping up and wiping her hand across the front of her jumper. "I'm soaking wet!"

The note fell on top of the desk. Meg watched in horror as the water soaked into Miss McConnell's blotter, the dark circle getting larger and larger.

Meg moaned and stared at the huge circle, wishing she could jump inside its center and disappear. She grabbed a handful of tissues and dabbed at the desk. Then she heard the classroom door open and willed herself to stay calm and turn around.

"I . . . I accidently spilled your water," Gaelen said quickly, wiping both hands on her jumper. "I'm sorry . . . I mean I am really *sorry*, Miss McConnell."

Miss McConnell just shrugged, her shoulders barely raising an inch. "It will dry," was all she said. "Sit on the heat register until your jumper dries, Gaelen. You don't want to be sick for Christmas, dear."

Suddenly Meg felt so light she was sure she would float right up to the ceiling lights where she would gladly do a couple of flips. Gosh, Miss McConnell was nice. Her whole desk was a mess and she didn't even care.

Meg hurried back to her desk, looking over at

Gaelen as they both grinned and shook their heads. As soon as she slid into her seat, Raymond yanked hard on her ponytail, his huge tennis shoe kicking the back of her seat.

"Thanks *a lot,* Meg!!!!!"

Meg grabbed back her ponytail and pulled away. What was wrong with Raymond? She was just about to ask him when she heard Miss McConnell clearing her throat.

By the time Meg looked up, Miss McConnell was already reading Raymond's note.

Fifteen

When Miss McConnell finally lowered Raymond's note, she seemed to have grown. She looked like the side of a mountain. A volcano about to erupt.

"I would like to see Gaelen, Raymond, and Meg outside," she said darkly. She put her fingers to her throat and cleared it like the anger was choking her.

Meg kept her eyes down as she walked outside. She could hear Raymond scraping back his chair, Gaelen scuffling her shoes up the aisle.

When the door finally closed, Miss McConnell held up the note. "I am not going to even ask for the author. I recognize the first verse as the one being used in the Christmas skit at the mall. And the second one . . ." Miss McConnell's sigh practically rattled the paper in her hand. "I suppose *that* was for your own private enjoyment."

Raymond's hands were shaking.

"I think that the Christmas skit is bringing out certain things in you three that I am not particularly happy with. Not only because I was the victim in this case. But because I see the danger of *other victims*. Children who may not be able to handle your . . . your biting humor."

Meg twitched as though she had really been bitten.

"I am withdrawing my sponsorship of the Christmas skit," continued Miss McConnell. "As far as I am concerned, there *is* no Christmas contest. I do not want you three representing my fifth-grade class."

Gaelen's head jerked up. Meg could read the color changes in her face. The embarrassed white was being quickly colored in with red rage.

"You . . . you can't do that," Gaelen insisted. "We are one of the ten finalists. My mom already made costumes and . . ."

Miss McConnell already had her hand on the door. "Your parents may call if they have any questions about my decision. I'll be glad to share this note with them. Now come back inside and get to work."

Miss McConnell walked in first, her thick-soled shoes marching directly to her desk where she opened the center drawer and placed the note inside.

Meg, Gaelen, and Raymond followed, heads

down, no longer worthy to represent the fifth-graders of St. James at the Christmas contest.

It was as though someone had pulled the plug on the entire class; it was that quiet. Miss McConnell did not blast her whistle and announce the grim details of the talk outside nor stand on her chair and reread the note.

She went about her regular lesson plans as usual. She read a wonderful chapter from *Homecoming*. But this time Miss McConnell didn't even try to sound like Dicey. She just sounded like a tired Miss McConnell.

Miss McConnell didn't yell or look sorry for herself or frown at Meg, Raymond, and Gaelen. She acted as if reading those awful things about herself didn't bother her a bit.

She acted like she didn't care.

Not caring hurt more than if Miss McConnell had cracked the yardstick against the side of her desk and waved it around in the air like a maniac, shouting that *this* fifth grade was the absolute worst in her teaching career.

The tiny bit of Christmas spirit that had flickered inside Meg went out, leaving a pale little wisp of hopelessness in its place.

By the time lunch was called, Meg had a splitting headache. In the cafeteria she sipped her milk and listened as Gaelen ranted and raved about how upset her mother was going to be when she heard they had been kicked out of the Christmas contest by Miss McConnell.

"My parents will be furious if they find out about that awful note," Meg said.

"Well, my mother spent twenty or thirty bucks of her own money on those costumes," Gaelen pointed out, chewing angrily on her peanut butter sandwich. "And my dad has been charging up the VCR camera for the past week so he could record us."

Raymond bit into a chocolate from the basket he had brought in for Miss McConnell. "Man, my parents are going to hit the ceiling. My mom said that my sense of humor would get me in trouble one day, and that day is here."

Meg pushed her sandwich away. "I should have ripped up the note at my desk. I feel so awful. It's all my fault."

Raymond rolled a caramel toward Meg. "Nah, I was the jerk for asking you to read it in class. I just thought it was so weird that I wrote it when we thought Miss McConnell was mean, and then she turned out kind of cool, and . . ."

Gaelen drummed her fingers against the table. "It was an act. She is *mean* on the inside, all right. She has no right to make us quit the contest. It's none of her business. Why can't we just stay after school or scrub the floor with a toothbrush for our punishment?"

"The whole contest went through the schools. Sister Mary Louise sent in our school banner and everything. If our own teacher is ashamed of us . . ." Meg's voice sank and then stopped.

Gaelen snapped a pretzel and waved the rest like a sword. "I say this means war. The Christmas present boycott is on. I'll tell everyone *not* to bring in a present for Scrooge. Scrooge is out and Mrs. Jackson can come to the contest and sponsor us."

"But Mrs. Jackson isn't our teacher," reminded Raymond.

"Well, Miss McConnell isn't, either," argued Gaelen. "A teacher has to like her class in order to be a real, true teacher, and that means Miss McConnell doesn't qualify. Maybe I should tell everyone to bring in a lump of coal for the old Scrooge."

Raymond nodded. "I can't believe I didn't rip up that note." He bit into another chocolate and frowned at the coconut peeking out.

Gaelen stared up at the ceiling and began to smile. "We are going to be at the contest on Friday. Don't worry, I'll find a way."

Meg sighed. She didn't even *want* to be in the contest anymore. She didn't want anything to do with Christmas. If she could just go home and go to sleep and wake up when Christmas was *over*, it would be terrific.

Raymond crumpled up the remaining basket of gaily wrapped chocolates and tossed it in the trash can. "Man, I think we'd better kiss that contest good-bye. I can't take any chances of getting in more trouble."

As the three of them walked toward the door,

Gretchen Barefoot, a sixth-grader from upstairs, came rushing into the cafeteria. She was running so fast she collided right into Raymond and Meg.

"Hey, slow down, lady," laughed Raymond. "Don't damage the merchandise."

Gretchen smiled and fanned herself with her hands. "Sorry, but I just talked to my mom at the hospital. She's a nurse and . . ." Gretchen let out a squeal of happiness and grabbed Meg's arm. "Guess what? Mrs. Jackson had a baby girl this morning! She named her Holly, isn't that great?"

Gretchen flashed past them, running down the cafeteria and calling out the news like Paul Revere.

"A little girl." Meg smiled. At least there was some good news to bring home. Too bad there wasn't more to go around.

Sixteen

The stinging cold against Meg's cheeks on the way home reminded her of the invisible wall of ice that had gone up in the fifth grade. The fifth-graders on one side, Miss McConnell alone on the other. Gaelen had spent the whole afternoon telling everyone about Miss McConnell kicking them out of the contest.

Meg walked slowly through the drifting piles of snow leading to the front porch.

She pushed open the door and Buttons ran outside between her legs, barely making it to the bottom of the porch before he lifted his leg. Meg waited for him and the two of them went inside. "Where's Pop, Buttons?" asked Meg. The house was dark and quiet. She hung up her coat and sat on the bottom step to rub his tummy. Meg glanced up at the bare banister, narrowing her eyes and trying to picture it wrapped with greens and bright red plaid bows. Maybe she and Lizzie could collect some greens from the ground when they went to pick out Mom's blue spruce. If they had enough, they could put some on top of the mantel and scatter some of Lizzie's pinecones.

Meg tiptoed upstairs, peeking in at Pop. His mouth was open, snoring. Meg carefully closed the door. No need to wake him just yet. He'd better save all his strength for going to buy the tree.

Thinking of the blue spruce energized Meg. She almost danced down the stairs, running into the kitchen and popping some corn. She carried the big bowl into the living room and started taking down the decorations from the artificial tree. So what if they couldn't be in the Christmas contest. At least Christmas had finally arrived at the Stafford house. The tree would start things going.

"No offense, tree." She laughed. "But you are going back in the box where you belong. The Staffords always have a blue spruce."

When Lizzie stomped in, kicking snow and talking a mile a minute, Meg gave her a quick snack and put her to work. Together they packaged up the tree and carried it to the second floor. Meg wanted the tree as far away from the living room as possible. Next, they pushed the couch off to the side, making room for the new tree in front of the large bay window.

Pretty soon, both girls were humming "Jingle Bells" and laughing.

105

Lizzie swept the bare floor and Meg lugged the large metal tree stand in from the garage.

"Are you sure Mommy will like the new tree?" asked Lizzie. She glanced out the window and looked worried. "She doesn't like standing on her feet to pay for . . . for . . . extratravaments."

Meg giggled. "Extravagances . . . and I think Mom will know this is our Christmas present to her. A blue spruce is a Stafford tradition."

Lizzie nodded, smiling again. "And my wreaths!"

Meg set the glass ornaments on the coffee table and handed Lizzie the old wooden Santa that had been Nana's when she was a little girl.

"You set Santa in the middle of the mantel so he can watch us work, and I'll go wake up Pop."

Lizzie stood on top of the piano bench and set Santa next to the large brass clock. "There you go, Santa. We will be back real soon with a real, live Christmas tree. It smells good all by itself."

Meg took the stairs two at a time. Pop should be really rested by now. He could warm up the car while Meg and Lizzie shoveled a path to it. They had to get the tree before Mom came home.

Meg rapped twice on the door and then walked in. Pop was lying in bed, his eyes open, just staring at the light fixture overhead.

"Hi, Pop. Lizzie and I have the living room all set up for the tree. We're going to start shoveling so why don't you come down and get ready to go? You can find some string to tie the tree, and warm up the car."

Pop pulled himself up, swinging his legs to the side of the bed. "Sure, Meggie. I'll be right down. Just give me a minute."

Meg walked briskly across the floor, pulling up each shade. Pop sounded like he was a hundred and five.

"Want me to get your boots, Pop?" asked Meg. She bit her lip, trying not to get impatient. Pop was just sitting there like he couldn't move.

"Your mother called today . . ." Pop rubbed his face hard with his hand like he was trying to wake up. "She said she found Lizzie's Christmas list and read it. She doesn't want us trying to get the blue spruce for Christmas, Meg. She doesn't want us using any of the money she has already saved for Christmas."

"What?"

Pop looked up, his smile never even curling his lips. "She's worried about money."

"Well, I'm worried about *Christmas!*" snapped Meg. "Nobody but Lizzie seems to care that Christmas is only a few days away. We have a dumb tree, no presents, no Christmas cookies . . ." Meg let a fat tear roll down her cheek.

Pop reached out his hand but Meg took a quick step back. She didn't want him to hug her and promise her that things would be all right. Things would never be all right if they didn't start getting ready for Christmas. How was the Christmas spirit ever going to come if nobody tried? "Well, I think we should get the tree, and if Mom doesn't like it, then too bad," cried Meg.

Pop frowned. "Meg . . ."

"I mean it," insisted Meg. She walked back to the door. "Lizzie and I are going to shovel the driveway. You should start the car." Meg paused. "Too bad I'm not sixteen or I could do *that* for myself, too." Meg stormed down the stairs, stomping each foot as hard as she could.

Lizzie was waiting at the bottom, her eyes two frightened saucers.

"Come on, Lizzie," ordered Meg, grabbing her jacket and mittens. She saw the ugly green scarf dangling from the hook and left it. Meg slammed the door and grabbed her shovel. Within minutes she was heaving little mounds of snow to the left and right as she wove an uneven path to the driveway.

"Boy are you fast!" laughed Lizzie, leaning on her shovel. "You should be a snow plow lady."

Meg didn't even look up. Scoop, lift, scoop, lift, scoop, lift . . . Meg's breathing grew fast and sweat poured in a warm trickle down her back. Any minute now Pop would be coming out the door. Any minute now . . .

By the time the driveway was almost cleared, the sun broke through. Meg looked upstairs at her parents' bedroom window, hoping to see Pop motioning that he would be right down, and they would all pile in the car to get the tree.

Meg squinted against the afternoon sun, shielding her hand with her wet mitten. Pop's shades were pulled down and the front door didn't open again until Meg and Lizzie got so cold they couldn't wait any longer.

Pop stayed upstairs and Meg grilled Lizzie a cheese sandwich.

It wasn't until Lizzie had fallen asleep in the big chair by the fireplace that Meg moved the couch back in front of the window. Then she took Santa down from the mantel and put him in the back of the closet.

Seventeen

"*Meg . . . Meg!*" Meg felt the reindeer tossing her back with his antlers, shaking her till her green scarf got tangled and grew tighter and tighter and tighter around her neck.

"*Meg!*"

Mrs. Stafford shook Meg's shoulder again, bending down and brushing the hair back from Meg's face. "Honey, it's Mom." Mrs. Stafford turned on a light. "This is my night off."

Meg yawned and stretched. "Oh, hi, Mom. What time is it?"

Mrs Stafford walked over to the chair, still in her coat and gloves and shook Lizzie. "Six-fifteen. Wake up, Little Lizard. Gosh, how long have you girls been asleep? It's already dark outside."

Meg laughed. She must have shoveled harder than she had realized. She couldn't remember the last time she had fallen asleep during the afternoon. "I don't know. I shoveled the walk, Mom."

Mrs. Stafford pulled a drowsy Lizzie onto her lap and blew Meg a kiss. "Thanks, it looks wonderful. Where is your father?"

Meg rolled her eyes upward and frowned. "He sleeps too much, Mom."

Her mother nodded. "He told me today he is going to try and cut down on the pain pills. Maybe that will help. We all have to be patient."

Mrs. Stafford leaned back in her chair and looked around the room, smiling.

"I love this room, don't you?" She glanced at the bookshelves Pop had built last year, the tall narrow windows on the side. "Where's the tree?" Mrs. Stafford slid Lizzie off her lap and stood up quickly. "What did you do with our Christmas tree?"

Meg and Lizzie locked eyes. Lizzie put a pillow in front of her face.

"Oh, the tin one?" asked Meg.

Mrs. Stafford frowned. "Yes, Meg. Our lovely tin tree. Where is it?"

Lizzie pulled the pillow away and stood up, pulling on her mother's coat sleeve. "We had to make room for the one Santa is bringing you, Mom."

Mrs. Stafford shook her head and looked across the room at Meg as if the whole tree business was her fault.

Meg looked down at her jumper and ran her

111

fingers along the smooth red line of her plaid.

"Meg, I want to talk to you about this after dinner," said Mrs. Stafford quietly.

Dinner? Meg hopped up, cutting in front of her mother as she raced to the kitchen. She had completely forgotten about putting the meat loaf in the oven.

"Oh, Meg." Mrs. Stafford groaned. She flicked on the kitchen light and groaned again. "All right, get out the peanut butter and jelly, girls."

Lizzie laughed. "We can pretend it's lunch."

As Meg lined up the bread, she looked up at the clock. "Oh, Mom, Mrs. Jackson had a baby girl this morning. She named her Holly."

Mrs. Stafford filled the teakettle and smiled back at Meg. "Isn't that nice."

"Can we go see her tonight? Raymond and Gaelen are coming over . . ."

The doorbell rang three times.

". . . now," finished Meg weakly.

"I'll get it!" cried Lizzie.

Mrs. Stafford banged the kettle down, but she was still smiling at Meg. "Oh, I don't know, honey. The roads are really getting slippery. Can't we go tomorrow night?"

"But the baby is so brand-new, and we are dying to see her, Mom. We won't even bother Mrs. Jackson. We'll peek at the baby, and you and Lizzie can wait in the car. Please? Mrs. Jackson invited us before she left."

Lizzie marched back into the kitchen with Gaelen and Raymond following behind. Raymond pulled a basket of chocolate candies out from behind his back. "Gram sent this over for you, Mrs. Stafford. Merry Christmas."

"Thank you, Raymond. I love Gram's chocolates!"

Gaelen reached in the fancy red bag she was carrying and pulled out a huge tin. "Christmas cookies! I helped make them, so they are delicious, of course."

Mrs. Stafford broke into a huge smile and hugged Gaelen and Raymond. "How very thoughtful. Please thank your families."

Meg saw her mother's face grow pink. Was she embarrassed she didn't have anything to give them? Last year there were two large Santa candles under the tree for Gaelen and Raymond.

"Thank *you* for offering to take us to see Mrs. Jackson's baby," laughed Gaelen. "We will be the first kids in the school to see her. That's what I call a *real* present."

Raymond pulled out a pink rattle with a scrawny-looking ribbon on it. "I found this in my little sister's toy box and washed it off."

Meg quickly opened the cookie tin and showed her mom how good everything looked. Surely her mother couldn't say no to them now.

"We were just about to have a quick sandwich," said Mrs. Stafford. "Someone, who will remain nameless, forgot to put in the meat loaf."

Everyone laughed, and soon they were all sitting around the table watching Mrs. Stafford and Meg make sandwiches.

"Lizzie, run up and get Pop. I'm sure the smell of the cold sandwiches has turned on his appetite by now."

Meg looked across the table at her mom, proud she was so much fun with her friends. Maybe now would be a good time to tell her about the problem with Miss McConnell and the Christmas contest.

"Mom, there's been a little problem at school," began Meg. "The Christmas contest . . ."

Raymond kicked her under the table and Gaelen clenched both hands together until her knuckles bulged out like marbles.

"What problem?" Mrs. Stafford looked up from the sandwiches.

"Pop isn't up there," said Lizzie, rushing back into the room. "But at least he made the bed."

Mrs. Stafford's knife froze in midair. "He isn't up there? Of course he is, Lizzie. Did you check the bathroom?"

"Yep, and my room, too." Lizzie walked over to the sink and pulled herself up to peer outside the kitchen window. "He's not outside playing, either."

Mrs. Stafford pushed back her chair so fast it clattered backwards onto the floor. She pushed open the door to the mud room and poked her head inside.

"His coat and boots are gone," she said nervously. "Where could he have gone? Lizzie, Meg, did your father say anything?"

Lizzie walked over and calmly took a bite of her sandwich. "Yes, he said he had a fever from being in this cabin. I bet he went Christmas shopping."

Mrs. Stafford yanked her coat from the mud room and tossed Meg and Lizzie theirs. She looked out the window. "Good heavens. The car is still out back. Oh, my gosh, I have both sets of car keys! What if he needed the car? We've got to find him."

Gaelen and Raymond both stood up, and looked down at Meg. "Maybe we should call our parents to come pick us up," suggested Gaelen.

Raymond looked embarrassed. "Mine went shopping, but I can stay here by myself. It's okay."

Mrs. Stafford tried to smile, but then just covered her eyes with a trembling hand for a minute. "No, no, let me think . . . I'll drop you three off at the hospital and . . ." She cleared her throat and smiled as she took Lizzie's hand. "And then Lizzie and I will go get Mr. Stafford and pick you up."

Meg could barely zip her jacket, her hands were beginning to shake. "But what if you can't find him? Maybe I should come and help look."

Mrs. Stafford pulled Lizzie's hat down over her ears and shook her head. "I've been married to that man for almost fifteen years. I don't think I'll have too much trouble finding that stubborn Irishman."

Everyone laughed extra hard. But it was a hollow laugh, like it was made of thin ice and liable to crack into a thousand pieces any minute.

Meg, Raymond, and Gaelen sat in the backseat on the ride over to the hospital. The roads were icy, and Mrs. Stafford almost slid into a stop sign at the bottom of the hill.

But nobody said a word. Everyone was looking out a different window, staring at Christmas lights flashing from roof edges and porches, and large white snowmen looming from the shadowy front yards. Meg strained against her seat belt and stared out into the night until her eyes got watery and she had to rub them hard.

Christmas music was playing softly from the radio but Meg could barely hear past her own heart pounding beneath her jacket. The night was cold and dark and the snow was starting to fall heavily again. Pop was outside somewhere all alone, thinking that he wouldn't be missed by anyone.

Meg chewed on the end of her scarf and prayed every prayer she knew, missing Pop so much it hurt.

Eighteen

Meg watched from the glass doors of the hospital lobby until her mother's station wagon pulled away. Maybe she should have stayed and helped look for Pop. She had tried, but her mother practically pushed her from the car and said the fewer people in the car, the better.

"Don't worry," Gaelen said, putting her arm around Meg's shoulder. "My dog was lost for three hours once and he . . ." Gaelen bit her lip and stopped. "Sorry, I guess that isn't the same thing."

Raymond jabbed Gaelen in the shoulder. "How you ever got in the highest reading group is a mystery to me, Gaelen. You say the *dumbest* things!"

Gaelen and Raymond traded silly insults all the way up in the elevator until Meg finally started to laugh. They got off on the fourth floor and walked right up to the nurse's station. Every time the swinging doors opened, they could hear babies crying and people laughing.

"Sounds like we are at the right place," Raymond said, wiggling his eyebrows up and down. "I hear my fans calling for me."

A large nurse walked over to them, sticking her pen back in her pocket. "Yes, may I help you?"

Gaelen went mute and took a step back.

"We came to see Mrs. Jackson's baby girl," said Meg loudly. "Her name is Holly. Holly Jackson."

The nurse looked down her glasses at the three. She did not look very pleased to see them at all. Phones were ringing and people were walking in and out the doors. "You have to be thirteen years old to visit without an adult."

Raymond nodded like he completely agreed with the rule. "We're very short thirteen-year-olds," Raymond said quickly. He took off his jacket and just smiled.

The nurse smiled back, then turned away. When she turned around again she looked serious. She picked up a clipboard and started reading it as though that might tell her what to do with the three of them.

"Wait here a minute," she said briskly. Before she got to the door, she turned back. "Are you related to Mrs. Jackson?"

Raymond stuck out his honey-colored arm and shook his head "Not directly."

The nurse tried not to smile, but broke into a grin.

When the nurse burst back through the doors, she motioned the three of them to follow her.

"Mrs. Jackson was our teacher," informed Meg as she followed the wide white skirt down the hall. "For over three months . . ."

"So I heard," replied the nurse. "Mrs. Jackson said she had the best fifth grade in the world."

Raymond took a quick bow.

The nurse stopped in front of the large window and pointed to the bassinet on the right. "I'll tell the nurse to hold the baby up . . ."

"Holly," reminded Gaelen. "Holly Jackson."

"Yes. The nurse will hold *Holly* up for you three to have a peek. Then I want you three to disappear *fast* before one of the *mean* nurses asks you what you're doing here. Not everyone understands how you can be thirteen and only in the fifth grade."

Meg leaned against the wall while the nurse walked away.

"That nurse liked us," Raymond said matter-of-factly. He held up the rattle and shook it in front of the window. "Hey, Holly — it's me, Raymond! Do you like my jersey, kid?"

Meg and Gaelen both waved and swore that Holly was the prettiest baby in the whole nursery.

Raymond knocked on the window and asked the nurse to please give the rattle to Holly. The nurse stared at the rattle for a minute before she carried it away with the tips of her fingers as if it were a smelly fish.

"Well, that was fun," said Gaelen. "We can write Mrs. Jackson a note tomorrow and mail it. We'd better not bother her tonight."

Meg pushed through the doors and hurried over and pushed the elevator button. Seeing Holly had been great, but now she could hardly wait to get downstairs and wait for her mom. Pop just *had* to be in the car with her. He just *had* to be.

When they got inside, they realized the elevator was going up. As they began to come back down, the elevator started to get very crowded. By the sixth floor, Gaelen, Raymond, and Meg were squashed against the very back. The lady in front of them was holding a brown bag that smelled terrible.

"Can you believe my Lenny refused to eat his liver last night and then hid it in his nightstand?" She laughed like her Lenny was a regular comedian. "Lucky I came tonight so I could take it home for the trash tomorrow. Too bad I didn't come last night or I would have eaten it myself."

The doors opened again and the crowd moved back to let in two men, both puffing on cigars.

"It's a boy!" laughed the first man, handing out cigars to everyone around him.

Meg leaned her head back watching the numbers flash down. It wasn't until the tall lady beside her shouted, that she looked down and saw Raymond slumped on the floor.

"Stop the elevator," shouted the liver lady. "This boy is having a heart attack."

"He just fainted," Meg shouted back. "Just let us out."

The elevator stopped, and the crowd parted as Meg, Gaelen, and the liver lady dragged a stumbling Raymond off the elevator and deposited him on a bench.

"Do you want me to wait?" asked the liver lady. "Should I go get help?"

Raymond recovered fast enough to shout *no* before the doors closed.

Gaelen sat down beside Raymond and peered into his face. "You're as white as a ghost."

Raymond gave a weak grin. "I doubt it."

Meg glanced back at the elevator. Raymond seemed fine. He got sick on roller coasters, too, and he'd always been afraid of hospitals. Besides, she really did want to get down to the lobby to see if her dad was downstairs.

"Do you feel like trying the elevator again, Raymond? My mom is probably waiting outside."

Raymond shuddered and shook his head. "I don't think I like hospitals or day-old liver. Man, there are too many *smells* in this place."

Gaelen let out a huge sigh. "Well, I promised my mom I wouldn't take the stairs since muggers love to use stairwells for their attacks. We'll have to wait for another elevator."

"Where are we, anyway?" asked Raymond. "It sure is noisy."

Meg took a couple of steps around the corner. She saw children walking down the hall, pulling I.V. stands along with them. Nurses were walking with some of the children, holding their hands and laughing.

"We're on the children's floor," announced Meg. "Maybe we can just check you in, Raymond. They can check your brain while we're here."

"Ha-ha," muttered Raymond. He dropped his head between his knees and groaned. "Get me some water or something. I really do feel sick."

Gaelen whacked Raymond hard on the back. Raymond sat up, pushing her away. "I'm not choking, for Pete's sake."

Meg felt in her back pocket for change. "I'll go look for a Coke machine. Gaelen, stay with him."

Meg grabbed a handful of quarters from her pocket and started walking slowly down the hall. The place was bright and cheerful-looking enough, but it still gave her the creeps. She had never been in a hospital before, except to peek at Lizzie when she was born.

Meg was almost to the end of the hall and still no machine. She looked around. If she could find a nurse's station she could ask for some orange juice or water.

She turned around by a large window and headed back. She would try to find a directory like they had in the malls.

Meg found a bulletin board as soon as she turned the corner. It was filled with notecards advertising used cars for sale or rides needed to Florida over Christmas vacation. Meg smiled at the photographs of happy children with casts and wheelchairs, waving at the hospital's exit. Meg knew she sure would be happy to be downstairs, especially if her dad and mom were both in the front seat of their car. . . .

Meg looked back to the left and reread a large sign on yellow construction paper.

FIFTH ANNUAL CHRISTMAS PARTY!
DEC. 20TH AT 7:00 P.M.
CHILDREN'S PLAYROOM . . . ALL WELCOME!!
R.S.V.P. MISS McCONNELL AT THE FRONT DESK.

Meg stuck out her finger and traced the last line. Miss McConnell? Surely that couldn't possibly be her Miss McConnell!

The double doors beside Meg flew open and a small boy ran out, a nurse laughing as she easily caught up with him and swung him up into her arms.

"Caught you, Buster! Come on. Let me change that bandage. What would Doctor Griffin say if she saw pink punch stains on your bandage?"

The little boy laughed and pointed back toward

the noisy room. "I'm going to miss all the funny stories from Miss McConnell. I like the reindeer jokes that Raymond told. He's funny like my brother Mikey."

Suddenly Meg felt light-headed. Raymond? Then it *had* to be their Miss McConnell. But she didn't like kids. Why would she be at a hospital knee-deep with kids?

Meg tiptoed back to the double doors, pushing one open a crack to look inside.

In the center of a brightly decorated room stood a woman, a book in one hand and . . . and holding a whistle in the other. Meg gasped. *Miss McConnell!*

Meg leaned closer, listening. She had to hear every word so she could repeat it to Gaelen and Raymond. They weren't going to believe it!

"And then the dragon with the purple hair said in his deep, deep, voice, 'What do you want for Christmas, little . . .' " Miss McConnell looked around the room and pointed to a little girl with long black curly hair. ". . . Peggy?"

The room exploded with laughter as the children turned to point and giggle at Peggy.

"Tell the dragon you want a kitty," called out a boy with an I.V. needle attached to his arm. "Or make it two and give me one."

Everyone laughed some more. But Peggy just shook her head and whispered something into the blanket she was clutching. More and more children began to talk at once, waving their hands in front of Miss McConnell and telling her what they wanted for Christmas.

Suddenly the whistle sounded, cutting above the laughter. Meg pulled her head away from the door so fast, she pinched her fingers as the door closed. Wow! Blowing the whistle at a bunch of sick little kids!

The room got quiet so quickly, Meg pried the door open again. Inside, the children were smiling up at Miss McConnell. Nobody looked as if they had minded the whistle a bit. Miss Mc-Connell was holding her finger up to her lips and smiling back at them.

"Thank you, children. My, you are so smart to remember about my whistle. My throat is still a little sore from my operation, so I don't want to use my big, outside voice for another month or so."

All the little heads in the room nodded up and down. A nurse standing to the left of the door leaned closer to her friend. "A little sore . . . boy, I heard the nodule they removed from her throat last month was huge. I can't believe she is even back here tonight. What a lady!"

Another nurse nodded her head and smiled out at Miss McConnell as if she were Santa Claus. "I wish we had another twenty volunteers just like her!"

"There is only one Miss McConnell," laughed the other nurse. "Remember two years ago when she dressed up as an elf in that green-and-red leotard and danced the fairy waltz with Chief of Surgery?"

"She's a big part of Christmas on this ward, that's for sure. Did you see that adorable gingerbread house she brought in tonight? The kids had so much fun decorating it."

Meg let the doors shut quickly, not wanting to hear another word about how nice Miss McConnell was. Every nice word reminded her how unfair she and her friends had been, only looking for the mean things and almost glad when they found them.

Meg didn't know Miss McConnell at all. None of them did, and they already disliked her.

Meg turned and started running down the hall. She would tell Raymond and Gaelen everything. But maybe it was too late. Maybe the fifth grade at St. James didn't deserve the real Miss McConnell anymore.

Nineteen

"No way, Meg!"

Raymond stood up and pointed to the bench. "You're the one who ought to sit down, girl. You're hallucinating!"

He finished his cup of water and crumpled the thin white paper into a ball. "Miss McConnell must have a look-alike."

Meg shook her head, pulling Gaelen onto her feet. "Come on then, if you two don't believe me. Miss McConnell is down there right now, singing Christmas songs and telling funny stories." Meg started walking quickly back down the hall. "She even told that joke you told the class yesterday about the reindeer going on strike."

Raymond smiled. "Yeah, I can sure tell a good joke, all right."

"Miss McConnell can, too." Meg shook her

127

head. She still couldn't believe how great Miss McConnell was with those little kids. It was like discovering that someone could sing or play the piano who'd never told anyone about it. Miss McConnell was funny!

Meg put her fingers to her lips as she neared the double doors. Pushing the door open a crack, she let Gaelen and Raymond stick their heads in above hers, totem-pole style.

Miss McConnell was blindfolded, swinging a long foam bat wildly around in the air, trying to hit a *piñata* that hung from the ceiling.

Children were laughing harder than ever as she missed again and again.

Finally Miss McConnell pulled off her blindfold and pretended she was mad. "Sure, go ahead and laugh. I bet no one here can hit this thing. All that candy will just have to stay inside the *piñata*. Too bad nobody here can help me."

Several hands shot up, waving. Miss McConnell blindfolded a little red-haired girl and pointed her in the direction of the *piñata*.

After a few swings, the bat made contact and the candy spilled out across the tile floor, sending the children racing to collect it.

"Gosh," whispered Raymond.

"What's she doing here?" asked Gaelen. "She's laughing!"

"I heard one of the nurses say Miss McConnell volunteers here a lot," Meg whispered back.

A little boy in a wheelchair shook his head

when Miss McConnell offered him a candy cane. "Don't want any."

"Would you like to help me cut the cake, Peter? I sure could use your help."

Peter shook his head again, picking up the tie from his robe and twisting it around and around his hand.

Miss McConnell bent down on her knees and pushed the hair out of Peter's eyes. "Can't I get you anything?"

Peter shook his head, his eyes never looking up.

"I'll help you write your Christmas list," offered Miss McConnell. "Since I'm a teacher, I know how to spell every word in the world . . . even *Tyrannosaurus rex,* if you'd like a dinosaur this year."

Peter was quiet, biting his lip. "I don't want nothing for Christmas this year." He looked up at Miss McConnell and then back down again. "I just want to go . . . home."

"Man," Raymond said, his voice cracking.

Gaelen stood up and backed away from the door. "Poor little kid. I wonder what's wrong with him."

Raymond and Meg stood up, everyone taking deep breaths like they had been underwater for a long time.

Suddenly more laughter came shooting out. Meg pulled the door open wider. Miss McConnell was pushing Peter's wheelchair quickly around the room as three other little children chased her with the large foam bat held high in the air.

"Help, let's get out of here, Peter," Miss McConnell laughed as they sped around the table filled with juice and cake. "The reindeer are after us again."

Meg giggled, glad to see Peter smiling as he held tightly to his chair and sailed past the door.

Gaelen and Raymond squirmed beside Meg, their heads glued together. Miss McConnell stopped running and gave her whistle a quick toot.

"Time for cake now," she panted. She pointed to the two nurses beginning to cut the cake. "Sit down, and we'll all listen to a story while we eat, okay?"

Peter turned around and reached out his hand to Miss McConnell. "Tell us about your funny class again. Tell us what they all want for Christmas."

Miss McConnell stood up straighter and shook her head. "I told you all about them an hour ago. I told you all about them last week! You don't want to hear about them anymore."

"Yes, we do!" laughed the children.

"Tell us about that funny guy, Raymond," giggled a little girl with a huge white cast.

Raymond nudged Meg. "Here it comes. She's going to tell them I get in trouble every five minutes."

But Miss McConnell just walked around the

room, doing a perfect imitation of Raymond giving a Christmas rap. It wasn't the mean one about Miss McConnell.

Gaelen giggled and yanked Raymond's shirt. "She does it better than you, Raymond. Maybe Miss McConnell should go to the Christmas contest with Meg and me."

A rattling utility cart squeaked down the hall, causing all three to jump away from the door.

"Can I help you?" asked the young nurse.

Meg shook her head. "We . . . we were just, kind of . . ."

Raymond grabbed Gaelen and Meg by the elbows and pushed them forward. "We were here to visit a sick friend."

No one said a word as they waited for the elevator. Meg pushed the lobby button again.

"Boy, Miss McConnell sure is full of surprises," Meg said at last. "Volunteers don't even get paid."

Raymond nodded. Gaelen pulled at her scarf and looked uncomfortable. "Well, she should have told us. . . ."

"Told us she comes to the hospital?" asked Meg. "Why?"

Gaelen shrugged again. "So we would have liked her more, I guess."

"Maybe she doesn't want us to like her," pointed out Raymond. "I mean, she volunteers to work at the hospital with a bunch of kids with real problems." Raymond frowned. "That one little kid only had one foot. I bet Miss McConnell thinks we're just a bunch of spoiled brats . . . two feet and all mouth."

Meg and Gaelen looked at each other. Raymond sounded as if he knew what he was talking about.

When the elevator jerked to a halt and the doors opened, Meg was the first one out. She walked quickly into the lobby, her eyes glued to the front windows. The snow was coming down hard, and the people coming in through the revolving doors looked like freshly painted snowmen.

Meg pressed her nose against the window and stared out, searching for Pop.

Suddenly a snowball exploded against the windowpane near Meg's nose. Meg jumped back, her heart beginning to race.

"Meg!" cried a voice from within the swirling snow. "Meg Stafford!"

Meg started to smile before she could even find her father in the snow outside. She ran through the wintry air until she felt his strong arms around her.

"Well, it's about time!" he laughed, squeezing Meg again and again. "We were about to send in the Eskimo dogs for you three."

Meg squeezed Pop tight and buried her face in his jacket. It smelled of icy cold and pine trees. Pop smelled exactly like Christmas!

"We were so worried," cried Meg.

Lizzie raced up and hugged Pop and Meg. "Did

you see what Pop brought us, Meg? Mommy isn't even mad anymore!"

Meg stepped back and shielded her eyes against the furious snowflakes. Pop wasn't holding anything.

"Look on top of the car," laughed Mrs. Stafford, coming up from behind and putting her arm around Meg.

Meg took a step closer and looked. On top of their station wagon was the biggest and most beautiful blue spruce that Meg had ever seen.

"Pop!" Meg spun around and hugged him tight. "You got one. You found us a tree!"

Meg was glad to hear both of her parents laugh.

"Your father bought the tree as a surprise," said their mom. "A real surprise, believe me."

"Pop has a job," cried Lizzie. "He made lots of monies on our wreaths and he made some more monies looking at blue maps."

"Blueprints," corrected Pop. He looked across at their mother and smiled. "I guess there are a few old timers left in Pittsburgh who still appreciate the Stafford touch."

"No wonder you were slowing down on those puzzles," said Mother. She reached out and touched Pop's cheek.

"It's a start," said Pop quietly. But he was smiling.

Meg reached out and hugged both of her parents, drawing them together into a warm knot. "It's a great start!"

Raymond took a few steps closer and bumped Meg with his elbow, both hands shoved deep into his pockets. "Hey, guys, can we do some of this hugging in the car? My feet are about to drop off in the snow!"

Pop started to laugh and soon herded everyone into the warm car. The engine had been running, and the heat and music pulled them all inside.

"I guess you're too hungry to stop for pizza, Raymond," said Pop, turning around to smile at the backseat.

"I said I was cold, not dead, Mr. Stafford," said Raymond. He nudged Meg and smiled at her. Gaelen and Lizzie both slapped a high five.

Meg laughed, too. She didn't care what they did. She wasn't hungry for pizza or cold from the snow. Every bit of her was just plain happy.

Twenty

On Thursday morning, Meg ran all the way to Chestnut Street, her green scarf flapping in the early morning wind. Each time it brushed against her face Meg remembered how happy her mother had been to see it on her.

She bent down her head against the wind and clutched a lumpy package close to her chest. Inside was a Christmas wreath for Miss Mc-Connell. Lizzie had added berries, Mom had tied some green ribbons, and Meg and Pop had supplied the varnished chestnuts. A Stafford original!

Gaelen was waiting for her at the corner. She reached out and shook the brightly wrapped present. "For me? I thought we were exchanging presents on Christmas Eve."

Meg laughed. "This isn't for *you*. It's for Miss McConnell."

Gaelen's eyebrows rose, one at a time. "Well, isn't that special . . ."

Meg grinned. "She's really nice, Gaelen . . ."

Before Meg could say another word, Gaelen held up a thin package. She waved it back and forth and grinned. "I even got her something! It's a pocket calendar from my dad."

Neither girl said another word until they climbed the stairs to St. James and pulled open the heavy wooden doors.

The heat from the school lobby blasted the girls as soon as they walked inside. A small table had been set up outside the office with Christmas cookies for the students. A little second-grader was biting his lip as he finished his sign for the table: HELP YOURSELFS!!!

"That looks good, Ricky," said Gaelen. She turned to smile at Meg. "Is your mom coming to Mass?"

"Both my parents." Meg started to laugh as soon as she said it. So much had happened in such a short time. Her parents had talked a mile a minute last night, like they hadn't seen each other for months.

"Well, it's about time!"

Meg looked up and into Raymond's face. He looked worried.

"What's wrong with you?" asked Gaelen. "Is your mom putting starch in your underwear again?"

Raymond crossed his eyes at Gaelen. "Hey —

we've got to do something. Only *three* kids brought in presents for Miss McConnell. I feel bad, man. I mean, we kept calling her Scrooge all last week and telling guys to bring her coal, and now I'm afraid they did just that. She rates more than three presents."

Gaelen pulled out her present. "I brought her one, and Meg did and . . ."

Raymond waved it away. "Yeah, so big deal. We were the motor mouths that got this Scrooge campaign going and now . . ." Raymond looked over his shoulder and down the hall. "My gram always told me my mouth would be my downfall. I guess I just never thought I would fall so early."

The morning bell rang out. Raymond and Gaelen walked on either side of Meg, their shoulders bumping against each other in the crowded hall.

"We were so wrong about her," said Meg slowly.

"Hey, there she is," said Raymond. He stopped and pulled Meg's arm. They stepped aside to let the other students go by. Lockers were slamming up and down the hall. Any minute now the second bell would ring and the halls would empty.

"Why does she look so upset?" asked Gaelen. "Move up a little closer so we can hear. She's probably complaining about us."

"Come on, Charlie," Miss McConnell was pleading. "It will only be for an hour . . . forty minutes if you're rushed."

Mr. Ross laughed and held up both hands.

"Hey, if my in-laws weren't coming for supper, I'd give you the whole night, Ruth. You know how much I admire you for your work at the hospital. But if I'm not carving turkey tonight, then I'll be an *out-law* before Christmas!"

Miss McConnell smiled and shook her head. "I understand. It's my own fault for promising those kids a special surprise. Little Peter just had a terrible operation and all those children will be in the hospital over Christmas. I guess I just wanted to . . ." Miss McConnell ran her fingers through her hair. "I'll think of something."

Mr. Ross smiled. "You always do. Don't forget to take those wooden whistles I brought in for the kids at the hospital. I left them in the office."

Raymond elbowed Meg. "Peter must be the nice little kid we saw in the wheelchair. I bet he would rather have a Raymond magic jersey instead of a whistle."

Meg smiled. "How many jerseys do you *have*, Raymond?"

"Enough." Raymond grinned back. "Enough to go around."

The second bell rang and the hall emptied. Miss McConnell rushed down the hall, stopping when she saw Meg, Raymond, and Gaelen.

"Children, you'd better hurry. The second bell just rang."

Meg wondered if she should give Miss McConnell the wreath right now. Maybe it would cheer her up a little.

But Miss McConnell was already staring down the hall, her lips set in a worried frown and a faraway look in her eyes.

Gaelen grabbed Meg's arm and tugged. "Come on, we're late."

But Meg's legs felt wooden as she walked slowly toward her locker, and her face wore the same frown she had just seen on Miss McConnell's face.

Now that her parents were happy and a giant blue spruce lit up her living room, Meg felt worse than ever for the little kids she had seen last night. Nothing could change the fact that they had to spend Christmas in the hospital.

She pushed the wreath into her locker and closed the door. Even if she worked all afternoon she wouldn't have enough time to make the kids a special treat for Miss McConnell to take into the hospital. There wasn't enough time to make them anything at all.

Twenty-one

Miss McConnell seemed tired during the morning. Twice someone asked her a question and she just stared out the window like she hadn't heard it at all.

Gaelen coughed three times to get Meg's attention. She looked worried and pointed toward the front of the class. Miss McConnell was just sitting at her desk, tapping her pencil against the globe with no expression at all on her face.

Finally, in the middle of science, Miss McConnell smiled. "Class, I just had a great idea and I was wondering if you could help me out."

Everyone must have noticed how sad Miss McConnell had been all morning because the whole class started nodding their heads as if they would do anything to cheer her up.

"I do volunteer work at the hospital," began

Miss McConnell. "Some of the children there are only in first grade. . . ."

Meg felt Raymond's huge tennis shoe thump against the back of her desk. Peter was probably only in the first grade.

"This year quite a few of the children have to spend Christmas in the hospital, and . . ."

Meg was glad she wasn't the only one who groaned. Even though she already knew, it sounded just as bad to hear it again.

Miss McConnell smiled and a little more pink came back into her cheeks. "It is sad to think they won't be going home for the holidays, but they are getting better, which is the most important thing. Unfortunately . . . I'm afraid I put the cart before the horse and promised the children I would bring them a surprise tonight." Miss McConnell held out both hands. "And now I don't have a special surprise."

A few hands shot up. "My mom and I made candy on a stick last night," Courtney offered. "They are cute little snowmen with red hats. I could call Mom during lunch and she could bring in a hundred. My dad said we made too much and the whole kitchen is filled up with them and he wants to know what my mom is going to do with them 'cause he said it would take an army a month to eat them all." Courtney stopped and swallowed three times. "I'll call at lunch."

Miss McConnell started to laugh. "Thank you, Courtney."

Patrick Frank leaned forward in his seat, shaking his hand back and forth. "Miss McConnell, I can have my dad bring in these really good popcorn balls. Popcorn is supposed to be really good for you, too."

Soon everyone had raised a hand and was waving it back and forth. The whole class wanted to bring something in for the kids in the hospital. Meg could tell that Miss McConnell was surprised and happy. It looked like she might start crying right in front of everyone. "I want to thank you all for offering, and if your parents are able to drop things off at the hospital, I would love to take in your treats. I've told the children so many funny stories about this class they feel as though they already know you. It would be very special if you would make them a card, something funny to cheer them up and let them know we are all thinking about them."

Meg opened her desk a crack and reached in for her markers. She would try to make at least ten cards before the day was out, maybe twenty.

Miss McConnell opened the supply closet and took out a thick stack of colored construction paper. "Why don't we just forget about the spelling quiz today and get started?"

Meg laughed and dropped her markers on her desk so she could join in the clapping. Miss McConnell sure knew which things mattered most!

"Hey, Miss McConnell!" Raymond was out of

his seat before Miss McConnell even looked up. "Did you say that hospital Christmas party was tonight . . . like to-*night*?"

A few kids giggled. Gaelen rolled her eyes at Meg.

Miss McConnell nodded. "Yes, Raymond."

Raymond slapped Meg hard on the back, then yanked her up by the arm. "Yeah, that's what I thought you said. Meg and Gaelen and me were thinking . . ."

"I," corrected Miss McConnell.

"You, too?" asked Raymond.

The class laughed and Meg looked nervously across the aisle at Gaelen. What was Raymond up to now?

"Well, we'd had plans, *big* plans for tonight but you're in luck, because now we're *free*." Raymond pounded Meg on the back again. "Isn't that right, Meg?"

Meg nodded.

"So how about if we three come down to the hospital and put on our little Christmas skit for the kids? We already have costumes, music, the talent . . . everything you need."

Gaelen shot out of her seat, grinning. She walked over to Meg and Raymond. "Meg's mom can play the piano."

The class started to clap. "Can we come?" a few kids called out. Everyone looked up at Miss McConnell.

But Miss McConnell was the only one in the

room who wasn't smiling. Instead, she still looked worried.

Gaelen locked eyes with Meg. Raymond started cracking his knuckles, something he only did when he was really nervous.

"Well . . ." began Miss McConnell slowly.

"My mom could drive us over," said Meg quickly. She watched for a change in Miss McConnell's face, waited for the start of a smile.

"Our skit is real cute now," Gaelen rushed on. "All about three wise men and how they got lost and then they find a star and . . ." Gaelen stopped to take a breath. "It's very religious."

Miss McConnell looked at the three of them. "I haven't heard . . . *all* of your skit. Are you sure it's suitable for the children at the hospital?"

Meg's face turned bright red. Miss McConnell was trying to be polite, but she really was worried. Worried that their skit would be as rude as the one she had overheard, worried that it would be as mean as the poem in Raymond's note.

"It will be cool," promised Raymond. He took a step closer and nodded his head a few times. "It will be great, trust me."

Miss McConnell gave a weak smile. "Okay. Thanks for offering."

Meg slid back into her seat, her knees wobbly, her heart pounding hard.

"Trust me." Raymond's words echoed inside Meg. . . . Trust me. . . . Would Miss McConnell ever trust them again?

Twenty-two

Meg's mother loved the idea of helping out with the special skit for the children at the hospital.

"I can't make it tonight, but I promise I'll be at the Christmas contest show tomorrow," laughed Pop. "I can smell a first place already."

Meg forced a small smile. She had put off telling her parents she wouldn't be representing St. James in the contest Friday night, hoping she would come down with a case of chicken pox or the whole contest would be canceled due to a sudden, terrible blizzard. She hadn't wanted to tell them before because things were already so confusing at home. And now that things were better, she didn't want to tell them and get anyone upset.

Meg and her mother sang Christmas carols in the car as they picked up Raymond and Gaelen.

Raymond's grandmother walked out with him, both of them carrying huge trays piled with chocolates and cookies. Raymond looked embarrassed. "Have fun, be good," his grandmother called out.

By the time they parked the car and carried in the cookies, it was almost six o'clock. A nurse behind the desk pointed to a lounge for the girls to use to change into their costumes and looked confused as she stared at Raymond.

"I thought all three of you were girls. Gosh, you'd better hurry and change in the linen closet over there, honey. It's almost time to start."

When Raymond finally opened the door, he was holding a mop in one hand and a bedpan in the other.

Gaelen groaned. "Oh, Raymond, stop with the jokes. I'm starting to get really nervous all of a sudden. What if I forget my lines?"

Meg patted Gaelen on the back. "You won't. We've rehearsed the skit so many times. We'll be fine."

Gaelen leaned her head on top of a stack of towels on the laundry cart. "I think I'm going to be sick — I really do."

Raymond slid the bedpan next to her and laughed. "You came to the right place, lady." Raymond twirled around on his skates. "I'm going to check out the audience. Better find out fast if they're naughty or nice." Raymond wiggled his eyebrows up and down and grinned at the girls.

Meg watched Raymond skate down the hall and peer into the room. When he finally turned around, his eyes were huge.

"What's wrong?" cried Meg. She and Gaelen raced down the hall. "Don't tell me *you're* getting stage fright now, Raymond."

Raymond shook his head back and forth as if he'd just seen a ghost. "Man, there must be a trillion people in there. I think I even saw a T.V. camera."

Gaelen groaned as she slid onto the bench. "Oh, boy, oh, boy . . ."

Meg heard the click of heels and looked up. Miss McConnell hurried down the hall toward them. She was smiling and wearing a pretty red dress with a green checked scarf. "Hi, children. Your costumes look great."

Raymond hopped off the bench. "Miss Mc-Connell, there are so many people inside. They know we're just a bunch of kids, don't they? I mean, you didn't tell them we're from Broadway or MTV, did you?"

Miss McConnell laughed. "You three are going to be fine. Meg, your mom is already inside. I'll start the introduction and you can come in." She pulled the heavy door. "Good luck, and . . ." Miss McConnell's eyebrows slowly drew together. "I hope that your skits are appropriate. We need a little Christmas spirit in here tonight."

The hall seemed too quiet for a few minutes. When the double doors swung open again a pretty nurse with jingle-bell earrings nodded at them. "Come on in, kids. It's show time!"

Gaelen reached out and grabbed Meg's hand as they followed Raymond into the crowded room.

"And here they are!" finished Miss McConnell. She joined in the clapping and handed the microphone to Meg.

Meg gripped the mike so tightly she was sure it was going to snap in two. Raymond nudged her with his elbow. "What are you waiting for?" he hissed between clenched teeth.

Meg smiled out at the audience. "Hi, my partner elf and I came down with Santa and . . ."

"That guy ain't no Santa!" shouted a little boy from the floor. "That's just a kid."

The children started to laugh. Raymond took a step toward the kid and pointed a finger at him. "Well — if I'm not Santa, then how come I know you want a new football and fifty or sixty baseball cards for Christmas?"

The little boy's eyes opened wide. He blinked at Raymond and nodded his head. "You're Santa all right, or a sort-of Santa."

Raymond grabbed the mike from Meg. "Now Santa feels real bad you kids have to be in the hospital for Christmas, but at least you're missing school. School can be a real drag at times."

The children started to laugh. Meg glanced over at Miss McConnell, who was leaning forward in her seat without even a smile.

Raymond tapped the top of the piano with his hand. "Let's listen to my new version of 'Jingle Bells,' okay?"

Meg and Gaelen looked at each other, too shocked to sing. Meg couldn't believe Raymond was going to sing this version with Miss Mc-Connell in the room.

> Jingle bells, homework smells,
> Let's dec-or-ate the tree.
> Oh, what fun it is to play
> Baseball and Mo-nop-o-lyyyyy

She could barely force out the words. Miss McConnell was watching Raymond strut up and down the room as if he were a time bomb about to go off.

> Jingle bells, homework smells
> School gets in the way,
> Let's throw our books into the lake
> And go outside and play.

Meg was glad to hear everyone laughing. She peeked over at Miss McConnell, but her head was down so Meg couldn't see if she was smiling or not.

Meg and Gaelen sang "Rudolph the Red-Nosed Reindeer" and "Frosty the Snowman." Then Meg's mother started to play "The Twelve Days of Christmas." Meg jumped, and Raymond and

Gaelen both looked at each other and then at Mrs. Stafford. Miss McConnell frowned and leaned back in her chair.

Meg tapped her fingers on the mike, wondering what she should do now. Miss McConnell had hated their skit for "The Twelve Days of Christmas," saying it didn't have the true spirit of Christmas, but Meg had never told her mother it wasn't supposed to be in the skit.

Behind her, Meg heard a clunk. She spun around to see Raymond lying flat on his back, his roller skate wheels still spinning.

The audience grew quiet. Miss McConnell and Mrs. Stafford both stood up from their chairs.

"Raymond's fainted!" whispered Meg.

Before anyone could move, Raymond started to snore. His thin little beard blew up in the air and down again.

A few children started to laugh. Raymond snored again and flopped over on his stomach. Mrs. Stafford and Miss McConnell both sat down. Mrs. Stafford winked at Meg and looked relieved, but Miss McConnell had a slight frown on her face like she wasn't sure about things.

Meg bent down over Raymond. "What do you think you're doing?"

Raymond opened one eye. "I'm changing our act. Miss McConnell hated our 'Twelve Days of Christmas' rap. Just wing it."

Wing it? Meg stood up and glared down at Raymond. How in the world was she supposed to make up an act in front of a room filled with people and a frowning Miss McConnell?

Raymond snored again and smacked his lips. The children laughed harder than ever.

"Oh, my, poor Santa has fallen asleep," said Meg in a loud stage voice. She tried to wink at Gaelen, who was standing there looking totally confused.

"Give him a shot!" shouted Peter. "That will wake him up!"

The children laughed. "Or take him down to the X-ray room where the table is so cold," called out another little boy. "They can X-ray Santa's big belly and see all the jelly."

Meg grinned. She looked over at Miss Mc-Connell. She was laughing now, too.

"I think if we sing 'Joy to the World,' very, very loudly Santa may wake up in time for presents!" Meg insisted. "What do you think, elf Gaelen?"

Gaelen blinked a few times and then nodded.

"I can't hear you, elf Gaelen," said Meg more loudly.

"Oh, sure," said Gaelen, beginning to smile. "Joy to the world, the Lord is come. . . ."

Pretty soon everyone was singing so loudly you could barely hear the piano. At the end of the song, Miss McConnell was clapping along with the others.

Raymond flopped over on his back and snored again. Meg shook her head. Raymond was real

151

good at never knowing when enough was enough.

"How can Santa give us our presents if he's asleep?" called out a little girl.

Meg scratched her head. "Well, I guess we have to use our secret, super-duper weapon."

The room got still. Meg tiptoed over to Miss McConnell. "When Santa is this tired, the only way to wake him up is . . ." Meg smiled at Miss McConnell. "A blast from your whistle, Miss McConnell."

Gaelen started to laugh. "A *big* blast!"

Miss McConnell tiptoed to Raymond and gave a huge blast. The children covered their ears and Raymond shot off the floor like he had been sleeping on dynamite.

Raymond took the end of his beard and rubbed both ears. "Wow, that lady sure can blow a horn."

He held up both hands and grinned out at the children. "Okay now. You kids have been real nice, and I have lots and lots of presents to hand out. But first we want to give you all one more song." He picked up the microphone and grinned at Gaelen and Meg.

Meg and Gaelen started snapping their fingers in time to the music.

"This rap is dedicated to all of you, and especially to our teacher, Miss McConnell," Meg called out above the music.

Well, ho-ho-ho and fa-la-la-la-leeee
you kids are a-o-kay with me.
Gonna tell you a story about we three,
then we'll cut the cake and trim the tree.
It's Christmastime and here we are,
three wise men searching for the holy star.
Looking in the east and in the west,
hunting hard to find the very best.

We've been to stores all over the land,
buying sweaters and Walkmans, as fast as
we can.
T-shirts, footballs, baseball cards by the
dozen,
anything, everything to keep kids from fussin'.

But holy stars don't shine over what's not
hot.
It took McConnell to lead us to this very spot.
We found you kids with your brave, cool
ways
being tough with shots and hospital trays.
Showing us all what's cool and right,
a babe without a bed was born that night.

Christmas in a bed or Christmas with a king,
It's who you are that's the number one thing.
At last we three are wiser by far,

thank you, Miss McConnell, for the holy star.

Raymond hadn't even put the mike down before Miss McConnell was out of her chair, clapping harder than anyone else.

"Aren't they wonderful?" Miss McConnell said again and again.

Meg felt prickles on her arms as she listened to the clapping and watched Miss McConnell move through the crowd. Miss McConnell was smiling at them, wearing a smile brighter and happier than Meg could remember.

"Thank you for that wonderful present," Miss McConnell said. She hugged each of them and then used the end of her scarf to wipe under her eyes. "Good music always makes me cry."

Meg laughed. Miss McConnell would smile tomorrow when she saw the Christmas wreath.

Raymond reached under his lumpy sweater and pulled out a wrinkled package. "This is a little present for Peter. Maybe you can slip it to him later, Miss McConnell."

Meg reached over and squeezed the package. "Feels like one of those famous jerseys."

Miss McConnell looked out across the room and smiled. "Well, you three should get some cake and then go home and get a good night's sleep. Tomorrow will be a busy day."

"Tomorrow," laughed Meg. "But it's our last day before vacation."

"Yeah," added Raymond. "I'll bet you'll bring in a cake for us, right?"

Miss McConnell smiled. "Right, and in exactly twenty-four hours I will be sitting in the front row watching you three represent St. James in the Christmas contest at the mall. And probably win. I never officially withdrew you, and I'm glad I didn't."

"The contest!" Raymond yanked off his Santa hat and tossed it high in the air. *"Allll right!"*

Meg squeezed Gaelen's hand. She was so happy it felt as if they had already won first place.

Raymond caught his hat and put it on top of Miss McConnell's head. "Looks good, looks real good." He grabbed Gaelen's elbow and swung her around and around.

"Merry Christmas, everyone," laughed Miss McConnell.

Meg reached up and patted the Santa hat, giving a tug so gentle that only Miss McConnell and Meg heard the faint jingle of the silver bell.

"Merry Christmas, Miss McConnell," whispered Meg. "Merry, merry Christmas to you!"